A ROSE MCLAREN
MYSTERY

MURDER BY STEALTH

LIZA MILES

Acknowledgements

Writing can be a lonely journey in many ways. Although the characters I am writing about constantly fill my thoughts, at the end of the day, when they are finished guiding the words of the story – it is their story and not mine - it can feel as if time has stopped. Their silence is literally deafening.

And, of course when I type the final words, it is by no means the end of the journey.

My grateful thanks to the many people who have cheered me on as Rose McLaren evolves as a sleuth in the world of cosy mystery.

Thank you Ann Chatterton and Hayli my beta readers, friends, my daughters, and students on the MLitt course at Stirling University; and to Mary Turner Thomson, who designs the covers of the books and patiently combs through the story as final editor.

They say it takes a village to raise a child. It takes a community to bring a book to light. Thank you to those of you who read *Murder on Morrison* and *A Game of Murder*, posted reviews, and sent me encouraging messages.

Scottish words used:

Aboot	About		Mak'	Make
An'	And		Mithering	Fussing
Ah	I		Movin'	Moving
Auld	Old		Nae	No
Awright	Alright		Naw	No
Aye	Yes		Nowt	Nothing
Baltic	Cold		O'	Of
Cannae	Cannot		Och	Oh
Cos	Because		Oot	Out
Dae	Do		Shouldnae	Shouldn't
Dinnae	Didn't		Tae	To
Dinnae Fash	Don't Worry		Telt	Told
Doon	Down		Th' morra	Tomorrow
Feart	Afraid		Th' night	Tonight
Frae	From		Wasnae	Wasn't
Greet	Cry		Wearin'	Wearing
Guid	Good		Wi'	With
Ha'	Have		Wid	Would
Hame	Home		Wis	Was
Havnae	Haven't		Whit	What
Heed	Head		Willnae	Won't
Intae	Into		Womin'	Women
Jist	Just		Ye	You
Killt	Killed		Yer	Your
Ma'	My		Yersel	Yourself

Chapter 1

Almost two years had passed since Constance Brown last opened the pale-yellow door of her self-imposed prison and ventured into the world outside. The silence of the deserted snow-covered street below echoed the loneliness of her existence.

"Dancing horses," she whispered, watching the clouds floating in the sky, above the window of her second floor flat. Their feathery wispy shapes stirred her imagination, reminding her how much she missed being outside and the freedom she felt when she was riding her horses.

Relying on local deliveries, sending gifts she could order by phone and keeping herself active on social media, she had managed to hide in plain sight. If visitors wanted to call, she claimed to be busy visiting elsewhere. She posted images of recent visits to The Botanic Gardens in Edinburgh, Stirling, Oban and various National Trust properties that had once been favourite haunts. No-one questioned why there were no pictures of her with friends or noticed that some of the images were out of sync with the weather patterns. Her friends knew she was reluctant to have her picture taken since the accident.

Hair loss had driven her even more deeply into hiding. Apart from Harry, solitude was her constant companion. She looked down at the brown wig and wondered if she would dare after all, it was such a generous gift.

.oOo.

Rose carried the two steaming mugs of tea over to the table inside the window of her shop, Muffins on Morrison. It had been a long and busy day and neither she or Trixie had had a chance for a break since the early morning start. Despite the dreich weather outside, the tiny shop was bright and warm.

"Och Rose, this is terrible. Did ye' ken aboot the auld wife? Did we no' send oot muffins fer her a few times?" Trixie looked up from her phone as Rose set the mugs of tea on the table.

"Who are you talking about Trixie?"

"See her, Constance Brown. Found deid in her flat. A' body thought she wis awa'. It wis the postie who called the polis." Trixie handed Rose her phone.

Rose put her hand to her mouth, "Constance! That's horrible, how could no-one have known? She wasn't that old, mid-sixties. *Old wife*, honestly Trixie. I really liked her, well not that we actually met, everything was done by telephone and email. She was a bit old fashioned and always very charming, appreciative."

Trixie wrinkled her nose, "Och, sorry Rose, wi ye comin' up to thirty-eight an all, I suppose a should be more careful how a'...."

Rose swiped at Trixie with a cloth. That'll do thanks, Trixie." She looked back at the news item on Trixie's phone, 'it says she was likely dead for at least two months. The last time we sent gift boxes for her was Christmas. I should have picked up that she hadn't ordered anything for Easter." Rose wiped a tear from the corner of her eye and pulled in her lips, surprised by the extent of her reaction. It wasn't like her to be sentimental about someone she hardly knew.

It was the day before Good Friday. The tiny Morrison Street shop had opened to a queue for their Easter offerings. She had created a beautiful baked Easter bonnet for the door and made dozens of dark chocolate orange muffins, mini carrot cakes and rabbit shaped biscuits decorated by Trixie with different coloured icing. Everything on display in the front and side windows had been sold. The glass-fronted cabinet and the shelves inside the shop which had been full of fresh muffins, cakes and more biscuits were completely empty too.

Trixie looked down at her coffee and wished she hadn't drawn her employers attention to the news. Rose already had a lot going on, worrying about what was happening to her father down South. She decided to change the subject.

"An yer all ready fer Saturday?"

"Yes. I'm looking forward to hosting everyone. It's going to be you, Rob, Marion from Glasgow and her new partner and DCI Chatterton as was - I can't get used to calling him Anthony - for dinner. Then, on Sunday I'll be going to Bristol, while they move Dad into the care facility."

"A former jailbird an' an ex DCI at dinner, och Rose, whit a hoot!"

Rose smiled. Trixie was right, it was going to be an unusual gathering of her tribe. The people who had become closest to her since she had had to change her life around. She looked at the old RAF picture of herself on the wall of her shop. It was almost as if she had had two lives. What would she be doing now if her sight hadn't become a problem? Would she have even passed the tests for NASA? Owning a muffin shop had been the last thing she'd ever thought she would be doing, but then neither had she thought she would go to prison or become involved in helping to solve a series of murders.

"Are ye okay Rose?" Trixie's voice nudged her out of her thoughts.

"Yes. Sorry, I was lost in the past for a second. Come on, let's lock up. I don't know about you, I'm completely knackered, and glad of the break tomorrow." A black cloud had hung over her since her father had been taken ill. She felt drained, robbed of the joie de vivre she usually felt around celebrations or holidays.

Rob and Trixie, were Rose's friends as well as staff and knew something was up when Rose announced she was closing the shop for the Easter weekend - giving them and Sally who operated the mobile trailer on Grassmarket the weekend off. Neither tried to persuade Rose against the decision. They'd learned from past experiences not to push her once she had made up her mind. They both agreed to take on managing the shop after Easter, so that she could visit her father in Bristol.

"Are ye needin' ony messages, Rose? Ah cin easily drop them o'er."

"Does that mean you're staying over at Graham's again?"

Trixie bobbed her head and looked coy.

"Good for you. I don't need anything, thanks. Have a good night. Say hi to Graham. Will he be coming with you to dinner on Saturday night?"

"Is that OK?"

"Of course, so long as he's prepared for a grilling - Rob will have a million questions."

"Aye Rose, no jus' Rob Ah'm thinking," she replied with a giggle, "nay worry, Ah'll prepare him weel."

Rose watched Trixie make her way towards Haymarket; she hated herself for envying her jaunty walk. Trixie deserved happiness and Graham did appear to make her very happy. "Come on Rose, get over yourself, no time for self-pity," she muttered, climbing onto the electric bike to make her way home to Corstorphine.

Two letters sat waiting for her on the table in the hall of the tenement. The first was from the social work department managing her father's case. Rose had had no idea how bad things had become for him until she had gone to see him last Christmas. It was the first time she had tried to spend Christmas with him, since before her mother's death. For years he had blamed Rose for that death. Now he knew the truth and no longer held Rose responsible; she had hoped they could mend their fragile relationship once and for all. To finally be able to get close to him would have been a priceless Christmas gift. She hadn't expected to be welcomed, but she would rather a cold welcome than the pitiful mess she had found. As Rose re-read the social workers letter, she thought about Constance who had lain dead and undiscovered alone in her flat. If she hadn't gone to see her father, insisted on travelling down, that would have happened to him too.

Rose looked at the second letter. She didn't need to open it; she already knew the contents. Her doctor had phoned earlier to talk her through the eye test results from the specialist. She had been legally blind in one eye for almost three years. And now, the other one was failing. She had no idea how much longer she would be able to see.

She started to make dinner and flicked on the television to distract herself. The local news show led with the story about the death of Constance Brown OBE, flashing up pictures of her as an equestrian medal winner in the Olympics and later, when she had fallen out of favour.

The reporter was interviewing a friend. Constance had sent the family a Christmas card, but she hadn't seen her in person since the accident. Rose frowned, it all sounded very odd. Why had no-one seen Constance in person for over two years?

Rose switched on her laptop. According to her public profile, Constance had retired from eventing in the early 1990's. Two years ago, she had broken her leg, an arm and her collarbone at a charity event when the horse fell. Constance had been accused of being reckless after the horse had initially refused a jump and she went back round the course for a second attempt. The horse only just cleared the jump and then fell, breaking both forelegs. The poor creature had then been shot by a vet who worked for Constance, in front of a horrified crowd. Constance was vilified by the press and public and removed from the charity she had started.

There were no public photographs of the woman since her fall and, from the news report, it sounded as if no-one in her circle had seen her in person for almost two years.

Rose tried to remember the last time she had spoken to Constance, but the intriguing puzzle would have to wait. Rose was looking forward to a long night without an alarm waking her, and spending the following day preparing dinner for her guests on Saturday.

Chapter 2

The array of appetisers and the spicy West Indian vegetarian patties Marion had made, followed by Rose's vegetarian lasagne, with salad and the bite sized lemon tarts she served for dessert had all been eaten.

"Did I make enough food for you hungry lot?" Rose laughed as she collected the empty plates.

A chorus of, "No Rose, still hungry," and "Where's the other pudding," echoed around the table. Rose was almost fooled when Trixie appeared from the kitchen and presented her with an expertly decorated cake covered in tiny blue and pink candles.

Rose laughed as she counted the candles. "Thirty-eight. Really Trixie!"

Rob started the singing as she bent over to blow out the candles. "What did you wish for?" he asked, while Rose began handing slices of the chocolate sponge around the table.

"Hush Rob, she cannae tell ye, ye great numpty." Trixie wagged her finger across the table.

Rose smiled and turned her head to look around the table at her guests. Each one of them had played a significant and important role in her life, since she had moved to Edinburgh. She had known Rob the longest. Their journey together through addiction had taught them the value of both trust and honesty. She had met Marion in prison, where Rose had served time thanks to her ex, Troy, framing her for fraud. Trixie had come to the shop as an apprentice while she was living at the young adults homeless shelter. And finally Anthony, the newly retired DCI who had barely tolerated but then appreciated Rose's involvement in his last two murder cases. Inviting him had been an afterthought and she was surprised that he had seemed almost grateful to be included. Graham and Mike were the unknowns. From what she had observed they were both good men. Perhaps she and Rob would be lucky some day and finally meet a keeper. Rose stood up and raised her glass of lime soda.

"I've given up on wishing. From now on, I'm making every moment count. Moments like this one, Here's to more of them and to you all. Thank you for being here and in my life."

"Slàinte mhath," said Trixie, waving a bottle of Irn Bru. Everyone stood and clinked glasses.

"I bet you never thought we'd be sharing a toast, Anthony," Marion nudged his arm and turned to wink at him.

He smiled. "I expect you thought the same, yet here we are, thanks to Rose."

"She's formidable, isn't she?"

"She is Marion, and a true friend. They're rare … valuable."

"I'm glad you think of her as a friend. She needs people like you in her life."

"Trust the only alcohol drinkers in the room to get maudlin," said Rose, overhearing the muttered conversation. "Enough, or it'll be lime and soda for both of you next time," she was laughing but her eyes dared them to continue. They took the message in good humour.

"Song time?" Marion nodded at Rob, moving to the sofa next to her partner, away from Anthony.

Rob was prepared. He lifted the acoustic guitar he had brought with him and started to play. His repertoire moved through his own work to folk and traditional Scottish songs that everyone could join in with. Saturday night turned into early Sunday morning before her guests went home. Anthony was the last to leave.

"Sorry about earlier, Rose."

"For what? For saying you're a friend? I'm glad you feel that way. To be honest with you, I need friends around me right now. With Dad and everything, my emotions are close to the surface."

"Everything? More than just your father?"

Rose pulled her shoulders up to her ears and shrugged. "The way that last case was just left. I know, in here," she placed her hand on her heart, "it's not your fault that the charges collapsed, you did everything you could to try and get that evil man locked up. Do you think he will ever face justice?"

Anthony opened his hands, "I wish I knew. The whole debacle made my decision to retire easier. If information ever comes my way that could prove there was wrongdoing, a cover up to protect him, I wouldn't hesitate to bring down whoever is behind it. Go to the Home Secretary if necessary."

"Careful, you're beginning to sound like me. You need evidence, not a gut feeling."

Anthony nodded. "You know it, Rose. Without evidence, no-one will listen."

"Right. By the way, did you see the news about the woman who was found dead on Thursday, Constance Brown?"

"Yes. What a tragic shame, poor woman. That postie deserves recognition for making a fuss and getting the police to check. It doesn't bear thinking about; her being alone like that."

"It could have happened to my Dad, if I hadn't gone down there and found him I mean."

"But you did go, and you made things right, Rose. Don't go down the road of what if's, should's and could've been's, he was the one who kept you at arm's length remember, even after your ex Troy and his mother were charged and found guilty of your mum's murder. Is that all that's on your mind?"

"Yes," Rose lied. Now was not the time to tell him about her second eye failing. "Thanks for coming, it meant a lot that you did."

"Ah, the life of a retired policeman is pretty quiet, I was very glad you included me. Happy Birthday. I've put a little something on your bed. I know you said no presents, but I think you'll like it."

"Thank you. You'll keep me posted if you find out anything about the other case? I'd like to put those ghosts to rest." Anthony nodded and disappeared down the stairs.

"Aww you lovely women, thank you," Rose said aloud to herself as she returned to the kitchen, grateful that Trixie and Marion had insisted on cleaning up and organising the debris and dishes while Rob entertained everyone with the music. She made a cup of hot cocoa, then went into her bedroom to unwrap the gift Anthony had left for her. A copy of Agatha Christie's Secret Notebooks, with a signed dedication by the author, John Curran.

"Lucky you Mrs Christie, all your murders were made up," Rose said as she flipped through the book containing notes and plots of the various murder mysteries Christie had written. She had discovered the mystery stories as a young girl, and the well-read paperbacks were still favourites. Even though she knew off by heart who the murderers were, she always found something she had missed before, a red herring or a clue.

.oOo.

Rose had just settled into her seat on the train to Bristol with coffee and copies of The Sunday Herald and The Observer when an announcement came over the tannoy.

"Due to unforeseen circumstances, passengers travelling to Bristol will have to change trains at York. We apologise for any inconvenience."

Rose sighed. The vivid dream of the carriage journeys that had disturbed her sleep the night before flashed through her mind and she shuddered as she remembered the details, watching herself in a different time, repeatedly gathering up yards of skirt material and being helped into a horse-drawn stagecoach by a man with a pistol. Each time she alighted from one carriage to a new one, the horses were unharnessed, then shot by the man with the pistol. She couldn't see his face, but she sensed it was Troy, her ex. She couldn't bear harm coming to animals, not even in films. As a child she felt traumatised by the agonising pain of watching Bambi losing his mother to the hunters gun. Her own mother had had to sleep with her for days afterwards, reassuring her it was just a film. Reading Black Beauty aloud, had made her cry in front of the whole class, the teasing and bullying afterwards had left their scars. But it wasn't the animals that most disturbed her about the dream, it was her ex. The fact that he still had the power to haunt her.

The Sunday Herald had published a double page spread, dedicated to the life of Constance Brown. The copy covered her success as an amateur and professional event rider who was awarded the OBE in 2000 and her charitable work. She had chaired a National Charity for the Protection of Horses and Donkeys, raised funds and opened several sanctuaries for them. There was a black and white picture of her as a young Olympic medal winner arriving at a ball, escorted by a Mr Harry Turnbull. Rose tapped her finger on his picture – she recognised that face. Rose took out her phone and typed Harry Turnbull into Google. Of course, it was because of Harry Turnbull that Constance Brown had become a customer. She looked again at the man's picture. There was something else about him that seemed familiar, but she couldn't place what it was. Rose sent a text to Trixie.

Thanks for last night. Graham is great btw. Mini favour when you go to the shop on Tuesday can u look up the order we did for the private party at the Strathallan Club, a while back. Under the name of Turnbull.

The paper had also published a photograph of a Canadian cousin – a man called Barrie Dunphy. The photo showed him holding up a Christmas card from Constance saying she was looking forward to coming to Canada for Hogmanay. But she had never arrived.

According to his online profile, Harry Turnbull was associated with a number of property companies investing in parcels of land and property all over Scotland and the North of England. He was also a major shareholder in The Borders Paper Company, along with Constance Brown. Rose clicked a link to Companies House. In 1979 Harry had held forty percent of the shares, Constance twenty five percent and two other partners had held the remaining thirty five percent between them until they resigned from the company in 2009. Harry was now the main stakeholder with seventy five percent of the shares. The record showed over £170 million in assets and an annual net profit of £13.5 million for the previous years. She whistled at the size of the numbers and then frowned. How could the most recent balance sheet, filed last year, show a net balance of £0?

Rose typed in the names of the two shareholders, William Summers and Donna Meikle, who had resigned from the company. Their absence from any online search whetted her curiosity. How was it possible to have no public presence on the internet in this day and age, even an accidental one, unless someone had deliberately removed everything? She exhausted all the possible searches she could think of and sent a text to Marion.

Thanks for last night, the patties were amazing. BTW, do you know how someone who used to be part of a public company can avoid an online profile? Become non-existent?

Rose knew it was the sort of information Marion would either know herself or have contacts with someone who did. It had been Marion's deft computer skills and criminal history in cyber crime that had helped connect the dots in the Morrison Street Murders, the first murder case she had tried to solve.

It was past 5 o'clock when the train pulled into Temple Meads Station. Rose took a taxi to the hospital and was directed into a private room. She hadn't known what to expect and was relieved to see her father sleeping and looking much better than when she had seen him last. Even though he now looked well-nourished, he was a shadow of who he had once been.

"You must be his daughter? I'm Doctor Sandeep. How are you?"

Rose jumped, she hadn't heard anyone come into the room behind her. Dr Sandeep was in her mid-thirties, her long black hair was pulled away from her face into a neat plait. She was tiny compared to Rose.

"Yes I am. Rose McLaren." She held out her hand towards the doctor. "Are you the doctor who has been looking after my father?"

"I am. He's a bit of a medical mystery, Rose. May I call you Rose?"

"Yes, of course."

"How he survived without medical attention after the stroke...-" She shrugged and then smiled warmly. "You were the one who found him, right?"

Rose nodded, remembering the day she had found her father lying next to the sofa in the living room, unable to move. The shock of seeing him like that haunted her and she was burdened with guilt. She should have stayed with him for longer, after he was admitted to hospital.

"I should have insisted on coming to see him a long time before the stroke but ..." Her words trailed off as the guilt stuck in her throat. "Something happened, we didn't really get along, you see."

The doctor nodded. "It happens in families. But you did find him and brought him here. You saved his life." Her eyes shone like pools of water, her face reflected compassion. "He's leaving tomorrow. The care home is very good, you shouldn't worry, look to the future, not the past."

"Can he do anything for himself?"

"He can walk, speak, and eat independently. He even has quite a sense of humour but it's his mind. I'm afraid he really isn't able to take care of himself anymore."

"Yes, the social worker explained that. Everyone has been very kind, helpful. I just know a care home isn't what he ever would have wanted. He was an independent and proud man."

"He is still proud, perhaps that's what helped him get this far in his recovery. You're not seeing him on a good day. He has been brighter than this, but it comes and goes. The care home will support what he can do, help him to be as independent as possible."

"If I hadn't found him, if I hadn't gone to see him. What would have happened?"

The doctor didn't reply. She put her arm out and touched Rose gently. "I've already told you, you saved his life. You were there at that time for a reason. I think you need to get some good rest. Where are you staying?"

Rose considered what the doctor had said. She was direct but her words, her presence in the room were comforting. "Bristol Grand, not that I think that it will be, grand I mean."

The doctor laughed. "It's not bad, you'll probably see some medics in the bar. It's a bit of a haunt I'm afraid."

"I don't drink." The words were sharper than Rose intended them. "I'm sorry, I didn't mean to sound so …-"

Doctor Sandeep held up her hands. "No judgement from me, Rose. I don't drink either. We soberites can be a pain at parties, can't we?"

Rose smiled. "I've been a pain both ways, I'm afraid."

"Well, good for you, that you decided to change that, I mean."

"Thanks, it's a journey."

"Yes. A brave one." Dr Sandeep looked as if she was about to say something else when her pager beeped. "Sorry, I have to go, I just wanted to meet you before your father left my care. Take care on your journey, Rose."

Rose watched the doctor make a scribbled observation on the chart. There it was again, those words, take care on your journey, as if she didn't just mean back to the hotel.

Rose wondered how her father had responded to her. His intolerance for immigration had been an increasing and ongoing tension between them since she was a child. Her mother had left the dinner table in tears more than once, when father and daughter engaged in a toxic exchange of words. Not only had he wanted a son, he had wanted a child who would follow his beliefs and views. Rose knew her mother didn't think the same way, but she preferred to keep quiet whenever her husband let his feelings known. Despite their differences, Rose knew the burden of responsibility, to make sure he was safe and well cared for, lay solely with her. It was what her mother would have wanted.

Her father woke briefly to eat dinner. He had no idea who Rose was and kept calling her Miss or nurse. His confusion made it easier for her to slip away and she was glad of the fresh air on the walk to the hotel. She had been right that the name of the hotel was more promising than the reality. The Victorian building was definitely closer to shabby chic than grand she thought, as she walked past the faded wallpaper and chipped paint on the way up the stairs to her room. She checked her phone. Marion's text came up first.

Yeah, u can totally disappear off line if u need to, but there's always a trace. Want Mike 2 take a look at someone. He's put together a programme for stuff like this. What's up? Mx

Thanks, that would be brilliant! I'm curious who these two are. William Summers and Donna Meikle. Owned shares in The Borders paper company.

Trixie had also texted and sent Rose a copy of the order for the Strathallan Club made by Harry Turnbull.

Don't be mad. I was at the shop today. I wanted to get a start on prepping. Hope you had a good journey. How's your Dad?

Rose opened the attachment. She had been right. It was through Harry she had started taking orders from Constance. Along with the savoury brunch muffins they had created a white chocolate and apricot cake decorated with nasturtiums and an iced Happy Birthday plaque, dedicated to Constance Brown.

Dad's doing alright. How many orders did we fill for Constance? Look for anything we shipped to William Summers and Donna Meikle.

Rose scanned the room service menu, nothing seemed particularly appetising so she decided to go out. She was making her way through reception when the television news in the bar caught her attention.

"Mr Harry Turnbull 72, a lifelong friend and companion of the recently deceased Constance Brown OBE, was found dead in his home in Musselburgh early this morning. Initial reports suggest Mr Turnbull hanged himself. A coroner's inquest, to determine the cause of death, will be held in due course."

"What the …" Rose said aloud.

"Are you alright?" asked the barman.

"Yes, sorry, it was the news."

"Ah, did you know him? Do you need a drink?"

"Honestly? A drink is the last thing in the world I want right now," she snapped, and made her way back up to her room.

Chapter 3

Rose had set her alarm for 7.30. Her stomach was rumbling, she hadn't ordered food in the room and she hadn't dared go back down to the bar. There was too much temptation. She reached for her phone to turn off the alarm. There were three messages from Mike, Marion's partner.

William Summers and Donna Meikle are brother and sister. I'll ping you their contact details in the next text. He's married, lives in Chelsea, two children She's a widow, no offspring, lives near Perth. Absence of information is weird, probably intentional. There was a Facebook account for Donna but it's gone. Shall I do more digging?

Thanks, dig away if you have time. Marion will tell you I'm a nosy baggage.

Yeah, cool. Lol, Marion described you as a curious cat. Watch yourself.

Rose smiled, she liked 'curious cat' much better than 'baggage'. Constance Brown's death and now the death of Harry Turnbull had piqued her interest, but for now she needed to focus on her father. As far as she knew her father hadn't made a will or signed anything that meant she could advocate and take care of his affairs. Despite Dr Sandeep's reassurance yesterday she was worried that her father's voice may have been lost when the final decisions were made. Rose wondered whether Constance Brown had made a will.

Her body ached and she had a thumping headache by the time she arrived back at the hotel several hours later. Her father's solicitor and the care home had given her a mountain of paperwork which needed to be read through and signed. "Come on, focus," she said aloud, longing for a real coffee and pulling a face at the instant coffee packet the hotel had provided along with a kettle.

She finished signing and reading the necessary forms. The only thing left from the pile of papers was the letter from her father dated the beginning of December. He had written it three weeks before she went to see him and had asked his solicitor to hold onto it. The solicitor hadn't read it, but he told Rose her father had instructed him to give it to her if he was unable to care for himself before he died and apologised for the delay in passing it on.

"I should have given this to you immediately after the stroke, but I was away when it happened and by the time I came back you had gone back to Edinburgh."

The envelope was addressed to her in her father's familiar cursive.

Dear Rose,

You know only too well I have never found it easy to talk about my feelings. The last few years have taught me things about myself I would prefer not to have learned.

I spent so many years blaming you for your mother's death, it took time for me to adjust how I felt about everything when the police arrested Troy and I learned that he had been the one who killed her. Because you had brought Troy into our lives, I still went on blaming you. I was wrong to do that and I am sorry.

Last week I saw my doctor and I now know I may not have much time left to put things right. Death doesn't bother me, but I have left it too late to repair the damage I did between the two of us, by rejecting you.

I know you want to come down for Christmas, and I hope I will be well enough to try and make up for some of the hurt that I have caused you.

If you are reading this letter it is either because something has happened to me, or I am already dead. If it's the latter, please no fuss. I would like to be cremated and put next to your mum.

I'm sorry I could not find a way to say this face to face. I didn't know how. That's the reason I have always put you off coming to see me. Everything I have worked for will come to you after I am gone. There is enough money set aside for care as well, if I need it.

Love, Dad.

Rose wiped her cheek and then ran her fingers over the writing, "You silly old man," she whispered aloud. The surprisingly heartfelt words in the letter touched her deeply. If only he had been able to tell her he loved her face to face. She looked around the sparsely furnished bedroom, the all too familiar escape route from her thoughts and feelings by drowning herself in alcohol was tempting her. She didn't have the energy or wherewithal to leave the hotel and go for a walk outside, but she knew she needed not to be alone, to get away from the temptation of the mini bar she had battled with last night. She took her notebook, went downstairs and sank into one of the bucket chairs in the back corner of the lounge. The bar was already busy and she hoped the busy atmosphere would take her out of herself.

"Can I get you something?" She looked up, recognizing the face of the barman she had snapped at yesterday.

"Sorry, I ...- Yes. Soda and lime please." She had been perilously close to ordering a vodka tonic, when she saw Dr Sandeep waving at her.

"Rose, hello."

"Dr Sandeep!"

"I told you this was a hospital haunt. It's not usually mine but I needed to see a colleague after we finished. How are you?" The doctor's dark chocolate brown eyes searched for signs of distress, and were penetrating. She looked different with her thick black hair loose, and a lot younger, she could almost pass for still being in her twenties.

"I'm, I'm ... doing better than when you met me yesterday." Rose hoped the lie was convincing. "Would you like to join me? Or is that a conflict of interest?"

Dr Sandeep laughed. "No, not at all and I'm off duty too, if you're sure. I could do with getting away from hospital banter. It can be a little," she held her fingers up in quote marks, 'sick' sometimes. I can't discuss your father though, that would be a conflict."

"Honestly it would be nice not to have to think about Dad for a while."

Dr Sandeep nodded and gestured to the waiter. "Bitter lemon, no ice please."

The women sat in comfortable silence, taking each other in as they waited for the drinks.

"Is that a journal?" Dr Sandeep pointed to the blue hard cover notebook on the table.

"Sort of, it's for thoughts and maps, solving puzzles."

"Oh, what sort of puzzles? I like sudoku."

"No, not that sort of puzzle. Mysteries mostly. Things that don't make sense when people die without ... Sorry that probably sounds very weird and morbid."

"A bit, but it also sounds intriguing. Cheers." The doctor tapped her glass against Rose's and took a long sip. "Ahh, that's good. Needed after the day I have had. How long will you be staying?"

"Tonight and then hopefully I can get the train back in the afternoon. Although, I might divert through London. My shop is being well looked after and they aren't expecting me back until Thursday night."

"Ah, your famous muffin shop. London? Do you have friends there?"

"You know about my shop?"

"Yes, your father talks a lot about it. How successful you are. He showed me the photographs he had taken of it when he came up to Edinburgh, after you opened it."

Rose breathed in and sat back. She was stunned. He had been so critical of her idea to open the shop. The one time she had persuaded him to visit, after Troy had been arrested, had been strained and he didn't come again. But she daren't think about that now and diverted her mind to the reason for going to London. .

"It's not a friend I'm going to see, it's someone who is part of the mystery I'm trying to figure out. About a woman who died in Edinburgh." Rose tapped the top of the notebook. "I thought, while I was South of the border, I might just see if I could meet them."

"Do you know them, is it dangerous for you to meet them?"-

"No. Actually, I had never even heard of them before yesterday."

The doctor threw back her head and chortled. "I can see humour runs in your family. But this sounds very macabre, dark, is that right?"

"Well, I'm glad you can see the humour but I suppose I am a bit macabre. May I call you something other than Dr Sandeep?"

"Oh yes, sorry. Kay, short for Ishikaa. Kay is way easier to say on the telephone. I think my mother had very grand ideas for her baby daughter. She was addicted to folk tales and romantic stories when I was growing up. Like yours, she expected me to bring her the moon, but I failed."

"What do you mean?"

"Didn't your mother want you to be an astronaut?"

Rose laughed. "No, that was me, I joined the RAF, it was definitely an ambition, part of a plan."

"Oh my God, I am so sorry. Your father would sometimes refer to you as the daughter who flew to the moon. He said you did it for your mother, to rescue her."

Rose shook her head. "Really. He remembered that I wanted to fly? He didn't even know me when he saw me yesterday, or today. Sorry, I know we can't talk about him.'

"I can't, but you can, if it helps."

"Thanks, but I can't, not yet. I have too many conflicting thoughts whirling round and round in my mind. Kay, would you like to join me for something to eat? I'm famished and to be honest, my own company is not good for me. Not that I mean I just invited you because of that." Rose flushed. Kay's intelligent stare was disconcerting, throwing her off balance. "I'm making a mess of this, aren't I?"

"A little. But I'd love to have dinner with you, Rose. Find out why you are going to London to solve a mystery and why you didn't become an astronaut. Come on, I know a great little Turkish place."

The two women talked until past midnight. Kay told Rose about her own fight to be independent, train as a doctor. Her two brothers were already highly successful lawyers by the time she was sixteen. Her parents expected Kay to agree to an arranged match which would further their status in the community. But Kay had refused and two years later found herself without support or a home to go to when she accepted a place at Oxford.

"Thank you for dinner, I'm very glad we met earlier," said Kay as she climbed into the taxi outside Rose's hotel. "Be careful tomorrow, if you do go to London I mean and let me know when you're coming back down to see your father, if you'd like to meet up again."

"I will. Thank you for tonight."

Rose stood on the pavement, looking at the back of the disappearing taxi. It was beginning to rain, she liked feeling the moisture as the drops of water touched her face. It felt refreshing, a bit like her conversation with Kay. Later, laying on her bed, she reflected how Kay had helped her stop thinking about the dark shadows of the past. They had felt so daunting earlier.

She checked her phone. There was a text and a photograph from Mike and a long text from Trixie with names and the information she had asked for.

Constance Brown started ordering just after we catered her birthday, deliveries to her home. Then, five regular Easter and Christmas boxes. None to Donna or William. The only order for Harry Turnbull was the birthday at the Strathallan Club.

Mike's text told her that through an online search using picture recognition he had found a photograph of a woman who could be Donna Meikle with Constance's cousin on holiday in Vancouver Island, Canada about ten years ago. Rose enlarged the image on her phone. It was definitely Constance's cousin, she recognised the man's face from the television interview. Alongside the cousin and his wife there were five other people – two children who looked about thirteen, and another who looked about ten years old, a young woman, and a younger man wearing a baseball cap.

There was nothing new in the news about the deaths of Constance Brown or Harry Turnbull. Rose sent a text to Anthony.

Hiya, still down in Bristol. Do you have any connections with Pathology in Edinburgh? Wondering if they have found the cause of death for Constance Brown?

She knew it was unlikely she would get a response to that text until the morning. From what she knew about the former DCI's routine, now he wasn't working, he was an early riser with no bad habits to keep him up into the wee hours. Rose signed up for a new online account with a service specialising in family trees. She input both Constance and Harry's dates of birth, but none of her searches yielded useful connections between Constance or Harry. She tried various other family searches trying to connect the names from the list Trixie had sent with Donna Meikle and William Summer, but she had no luck with that either. Rose registered her searches for updates in case she had missed anything.

She paused her pen in mid air - her gut instincts kept telling her something was wrong. Two people who had known each other for years did not just die within months of each other in unusual circumstances. And, even though male suicide was on the rise, Rose remembered that when she met Harry Turnbull she hadn't cared for him very much. He had been somewhat familiar with her and was very sure of himself. She felt he was an unlikely candidate for suicide - unless it had all been an act. She was about to switch off the bedside lamp when her phone pinged with a text from Anthony.

Nothing re the Brown woman. Sounds accidental. In the bathroom, slipped and banged her head. Why the ongoing interest?

Rose responded. *Because she was a customer who died in unusual circumstances.*

There's no mystery. Look at the stats, people slip and fall and die in their homes every day. It's a fact.

OK, good to know. Thanks. Night.

Night Rose. Hope things with your father are going as well as possible in the circumstances.

The shadows had started to gather again and Rose tossed and turned most of the night. Despite Anthony Chatterton's text the feeling that something was wrong with Constance Brown's death wouldn't go away. She knew herself well enough, if she went straight back to Edinburgh without at least talking to Constance's former business partner, William Summers, it would continue to distract her. Donna Meikle lived in Perth, so getting to meet her would be easier. She let the hotel know she was checking out first thing and booked herself on a train to London after visiting her father at the care home.

Rose's father didn't recognise her when she first arrived. She accepted his ramblings, assuming she was one of the care assistants. He told her he had a son who was a pilot and his wife would be visiting later. But, just as she was leaving he called her name.

"Rose?"

"Yes Dad."

"Tell your mother I'm ready for tea, will you."

His words were soft, almost tender. They felt good, and she understood, in the next moment, she would be a stranger again. Brushing the tears from her cheek, Rose ordered a taxi to take her to the station.

Chapter 4

Thanks to Mike, Rose knew the exact house on Smith Street where William Summers lived with his wife and two children. It was a pretty street, built in the late 1700's, off the King's Road in Chelsea. Rose tapped on the door, she was going to pretend Harry had given her the address, but no-one was home.

She walked back along the street towards Kings Road. There was no cafe nearby, just a pub called The Phoenix on the other side of the road opposite the house. She ordered a lime soda and settled in at a corner table outside. The location gave Rose a perfect view to sit and observe any comings and goings from the terraced Regency house.

It was just after four when two teenagers, a boy and a girl in school uniform, arrived and let themselves in. A few minutes later a tall and fashionably dressed woman let herself through the front door. She didn't look old enough to be the mother of the children. Rose thought she looked too well dressed to be an au pair.

"Anything else, Miss?" asked the barman who was clearing glasses and wiping down the outside tables. "We'll get quite busy soon."

"Right. Thanks, another lime soda and a menu please. Do the residents on the street use the pub or is it mostly tourists and visitors?"

"No, lots of locals come here. Anyone in particular?"

"The Summers family three doors down, the pale blue house, William ... do you know him?"

The boy looked away for a second, then turned back. "Are you a reporter?"

"No, I'm a friend of a friend, from Edinburgh. I came by on the off-chance I might see him, but he doesn't appear to be at home. Have there been reporters coming around?"

"Yeah, when his wife left. Just the scandal rags, you know."

"Right, oh dear. My friend didn't say."

The boy raised his eyebrows. "He moved the new girl in not long after, while his wife was in the hospital. The girl was a regular here, that's how they met. She's from Aus. Comes over here on a working visa and lands herself a millionaire."

"Oh, so did you know her?"

"Yeah, a bit. But she wasn't interested in getting to know anyone like me. Sorry, the landlord's giving me the evil eye, I better get back to work. Drink and a menu coming right up."

"Thanks." Rose took out her notebook and added the Australian girl to the notes she had made about William and put a question mark next to his wife's name, Andrea Summers. If the press had been constantly around, could that be why he had tried to wipe himself off the internet? Had it been nothing to do with Constance Brown at all?

Mike, is there anything about William Summers' wife anywhere? She left him about a year ago and there were press reporters buzzing around, according to the local pub. He has a new mistress living with him, an Australian girl. I'll try and get her name.

It was the landlord who brought out Rose's drink and the menu. "You've been asking questions about the Summers?"

"Not exactly, I'm a friend of a friend from Scotland."

"Yeah, well if I were you I'd steer well clear. I told the girl that, but he's a sweet talker. It's not the first time he's had something on the side, except that his missus didn't take off before. He was carrying on with the girl before his wife had the accident. Shame, she was a nice woman."

"Do you know where she went?"

The landlord shrugged. "Nah, I just heard that she'd had to stay in hospital for quite a while. That's all. Seen anything you like?" He pointed to the menu.

"Yes, smoked salmon salad and a baked potato. Thanks."

Rose wondered why the suggestion to steer clear? From the young woman she had seen going into the house, Rose would definitely not be his type. Perhaps there were more nefarious reasons. She was just about to try another search for the wife via the Daily Mail online when a man with blonde floppy hair and the sort of rugged good looks that would appeal to advertisers, seeking to tempt women to buy expensive outerwear clothing for their man strode past her table and made his way into the pub.

"There's your man," said the young waiter as he brought out her order. "Shall I say you're looking for him?"

"No, it's fine, thanks. I'll finish this first."

Rose wanted time to reconsider her story. If she mentioned Harry it might put William on his guard. She couldn't pretend to be a friend of his sister Donna, it would be too easily found out. She was still pondering what to say when William came out and approached her table.

"I hear you're looking for me, friend of a friend?"

Rose flushed. "Sorry, it was a bit of a tall tale."

"You're a journalist?"

"No, not exactly, I mean I'm not looking to do a scandal story. I'm doing research for my novel. My heroine is a student who meets an older man in London, moves in with him. I'm talking to different couples about their experience. No names will be used. I promise." The lie had fallen out of her mouth without a blink or a flush.

William raised his eyebrow, sat down close to Rose and leaned in. "How did you know about me, where to find me?"

"Umm Daily Mail, I think. I'm sorry I've been collecting all sorts of personal press cuttings. I'm not quite sure where I read about you."

He placed his hand on Rose's arm, and started pressing his fingers into her flesh. "That's because you didn't, unless you bought a copy of the morning edition, which I highly doubt. Now, what is it you really want? No way are you researching a novel." His warm breath, close to her cheek, smelled of ale.

She turned to face him, he was so close their noses were almost touching. His grip was firm and try as she might she couldn't free her arm.

"OK. Constance Brown, she's the reason I wanted to meet you."

His face twitched, her answer appeared to take him by surprise. He relaxed the grip on her arm and jerked backwards into his chair. "Constance? I haven't seen her for over two years."

"Why did you resign from the company?"

"Seriously? Why is that any of your business?"

"Constance was one of my customers. You do know that she's dead?"

"Yes, I do. Rather tragic given who she used to be. It's not the sort of death one would wish on anyone." He waved his arm in the air to catch a fly. "Gotha," he said, looking rather pleased with the dead trophy in the palm of his hand.

"What sort of death is that?" Rose probed.

"Being alone, not being found. Why? Do you think I had something to do with it?"

Rose shook her head. She knew she had been clumsy. "No. Of course not. Sorry."

William frowned. "How long have you known her?"

We didn't meet, not in person. She started ordering gifts at Christmas and Easter and for birthdays, from my shop, after her friend Harry gave her a birthday party which I catered. The party was before her accident. And now he's dead too."

"Harry is dead? When?"

"It was on the news on Sunday night. But there haven't been any reports about it since then. You didn't know?"

"We were out of the country over the weekend. Came back late Sunday. So no. Do you know how?"

"The news report said suicide, but ...-"

"But you don't think so. Who are you really? You're not the police. Insurance? PI?"

"Rose, Rose McLaren. I really do run a muffin shop in Edinburgh."

"Right. Well if that's all, Rose McLaren, I'm going to go home to my family. But there is one thing I will say, don't weep too many tears for Harry Turnbull. He wasn't the man he pretended to be. In fact I think he was the devil incarnate. Cheers Rose." He downed the last of his pint, waved at the landlord through the window and sauntered over to his house without looking back.

Rose bit her lip. That could have gone better, she thought. She pushed the half eaten plate of food to one side and went inside to pay.

"Everything alright?" The landlord was hovering on the other side of the bar. "William found you then."

"Yes, yes he did. Thanks for that. How much do I owe you?" Rose was tight-lipped. She knew it wasn't the landlord's fault that the conversation hadn't gone well, but she was annoyed that he had spilled the beans, she had been bounced into speaking to William before she was ready. The novel story had been stupid. William would probably contact his sister and warn her. She really wanted to meet Donna. To find out about the trip to Canada and how well she knew Constance's cousin.

Rose was swithering about whether to book herself on the night train when Mike's text pinged in.

William's ex hasn't gone far, Abingdon Mansions, off Sloane Street. You'll love this, the flat she's living in is owned by Harry Turnbull.

You're a miracle worker Mike, how did you find out?

I didn't. There was a press report with a picture of her going into the building. I just followed the trail. It's amazing what people will tell a perfect stranger on the phone.

You phoned her?

No, I phoned the security firm managing the building. They have a twenty four hour guard, who doubles as a doorman.

OK, I'll change plans and stay over.

A mate of mine has a spare room in Battersea if you need a bed. He's an OK bloke, let me know.

Thanks Mike.

Abingdon Mansions was an imposing red brick block built at the end of the 19th century. From street level Rose could almost smell the quality of the expensive furnishings and upholstery inside. The doorman immediately shot out from behind the wooden desk when he saw Rose walk up the steps, outside the glass fronted doors.

"Can I help you?"

"I am here on the off chance that umm," Rose paused, what if the Summers woman was using a different name? "Sorry, silly of me, I only know her by her married name, to see Mrs Summers. Is she home do you know?"

"Who shall I tell her is here?"

Rose decided to brave it out, "Rose McLaren, she'll remember me if you mention I'm a friend of Harry Turnbull.

The doorman shrugged and picked up the internal phone. Her gamble paid off, "Mrs Summers will meet you in the downstairs foyer."

She was admitted through locked frosted panelled glass doors into a sumptuous waiting area.

Some foyer, you could hold a ball in here, she thought as she settled into a comfortable upholstered arm chair. Rose picked up an old copy of Horse and Hound magazine, there was an inset picture of Harry Turnbull, in full riding regalia, on the front cover.

"Rose?" The woman standing in front of her was vastly different than the one Rose had expected. According to Mike's text, she was in her early fifties, but she had the demeanour of a much older person. Her shoulders sagged, her dress, albeit designer, hung off her thin frame as if it were several sizes too large and she was walking with a cane. Despite the carefully applied make up, her face was prematurely lined.

"Yes, thanks so much for meeting me."

"Sorry, I don't remember meeting you before. You are, or were, a friend of Harry's?" Her voice slurred.

Rose wondered if she had been drinking until she realised one side of the woman's mouth drooped. The way her fathers had after his stroke.

"Harry used to purchase things from my shop, in Edinburgh, so did Constance."

"I see, well I'm sorry but I don't want to buy whatever you are selling." She turned slowly, grimacing, as if every movement was painful.

"Wait, no, sorry I mean, I'm not selling anything. I just wanted to talk to you. About Harry, if that would be ok?"

"I'm sorry Rose but I haven't seen Harry since last summer. When he heard I was ill, after the accident, he was so kind. He lent me his flat. But now I ..., I thought you may have come to tell me if I could stay here or not." Her pale blue eyes filled with tears and her pallor under the foundation was fading, she looked grey.

Rose pushed herself up out of the chair and gently touched her on the arm. "I'm so sorry, I really didn't mean to upset you, I won't bother you anymore."

"I'll be alright. Hearing about Harry killing himself has been a tremendous shock, I haven't been myself. I'm sorry and If you'd still like to, please come up, make us both a cup of tea. It would help me to talk to someone else who knew him. He was a dear friend and I doubt I will be able to make it up to Scotland for the funeral."

"Really? If you're sure. Thank you."

Rose busied herself in the well stocked kitchen making tea and considered what she knew so far about Harry Turnbull. William Summers had been disparaging about him, yet, his ex wife, it seemed, had been close to him. Liked him. So who was Harry really, a devil or a kindly good Samaritan?

"Thank you. I'm not used to being so useless. Eighteen months ago, before the accident, I was preparing to run in the New York marathon." Her face was wistful as she spoke. "Then came the stroke." The light from the window, as the sun set, highlighted the lines across her face. The living room decor did not suit her soft elegance, it was minimalist and almost too masculine. "You say you knew Harry because he used to come to your shop?"

"He ordered some special muffins for a birthday lunch for Constance, and then she carried on ordering from me."

"Ah Constance. That's just like Harry, thoughtful. Was that the birthday before her accident? I was supposed to be there as well."

"You do know that Constance is also dead?"

"I do, Harry told me and then of course it was all over the news. Poor thing. I don't understand it, last time I met her, she was still such a social live wire. She knew so many people, why no-one knew she was there, by herself, I cannot fathom."

"Yes, that's what I think. The way she was all alone, after telling her cousin she was going to visit him in Canada. it doesn't make sense."

"Constance wasn't always … Sorry one should never speak ill of the dead should they? Why are you so concerned though, if she was just a customer?"

"I don't know really, it's just a gut feeling. I often have them, I'm afraid."

"They can often be right. I wished I'd listened to mine."

"Mrs Summers …-"

"Oh, Andrea please. Don't listen to me. I'm just being silly."

"What didn't you listen to?"

"The fact that my husband was continuing to have affairs, that my body was not performing the way it used to, that our financial situation was in tatters." She pursed her lips. "I knew about his latest fancy piece and the money, but I buried my head in the sand. I couldn't face the truth. I didn't want to."

"I am so sorry."

"Harry was going to help me fight for what was mine, but someone or something changed his mind. And now

Harry's dead, I will be homeless, destitute." Her hands were shaking as she put the china mug onto the coffee table. She hadn't touched a drop of the hot tea.

"But surely. I mean the house on Smith Street, isn't that a shared asset? It must be worth a fortune, the way house prices in London are nowadays."

"Oh my dear girl, it should have been, it was mine before I married William. But love can make you do foolish things and it's entirely his, or rather was part of his business. Which means he too will be moving. He's lost everything. Stupid man."

"Is that why he hated Harry?"

"Oh, How did you know that?"

"It was something he said when I met him."

Andrea pulled herself upright and jabbed a finger towards Rose.

"I see. I thought you came here as a friend of Harry's, not as a snoop for William. I think you'd better leave."

Rose opened her mouth. She didn't know what to say. She had been caught out in a lie, but not the lie Andrea was accusing her of.

"Andrea ...-

"Just go Rose, whoever you are."

Rose picked up her bag. She paused at the front door when she heard huge sobs emanating from the living room. Rose turned back towards the living room, where she had left Andrea sitting. "Please Andrea, I'm sorry I lied about knowing Harry. I am honestly not here as a spy for William. Maybe if you tell me what's been going on I can help?"

Andrea reached back behind the sofa and patted Rose on the hand. "How long do you have?"

It was past 10 o'clock by the time Rose left Abingdon Mansions. Her notebook was filled with her own version of shorthand whilst she tried to take down all the information Andrea shared with her about Constance and Harry and the business empire they had created together after Constance had taken a break from eventing. She had been sick and missed out on competing for another Olympic medal. Rose made her way to Kings Cross by taxi hoping to make the night train. She needed to get back to Scotland. It was more important than ever that she met William's sister Donna.

Chapter 5

All the sleeping cars were booked by the time she arrived at the station and Rose had to settle for a recliner. Famished, she made short work of the pathetic white bread sandwich from the late night kiosk. Then, spreading out her notebook she began to create a coded map, connecting the people and events Andrea had described to her. Creating lists that looked like a flight plan were Rose's way of figuring things out, she created complex patterns that to anyone unfamiliar with aeronautical mapping looked confusing.

Harry had been a friend of Andrea's father. Harry was much younger, but they shared a passion for racing and horses. It was Harry who bought Andrea a decent horse and encouraged her in amateur eventing, which is where she met Constance. According to Andrea, Harry had been very much in love with Constance, but she was not the marrying kind. Her first and only love was for her horses. Born in an age where marriage was expected, Constance bucked tradition but Harry had remained a faithful consort and companion, whenever Constance needed one. Andrea had said she was puzzled why Harry would not have been in contact with Constance after the fall and wondered if her death had been behind Harry taking his own life. Because he blamed himself.

It was through Harry and Constance that Andrea had met Donna's younger brother William. Despite their age difference William and Andrea had fallen in love. It had been Harry's idea for William and Donna to go into business with him and Constance.

Andrea had no idea anything was wrong until Donna and William resigned. William told her he couldn't work with Harry anymore, but he wouldn't tell her what had happened. Donna seemed to resign out of loyalty to William. The Summers personal money troubles started after William had taken a gamble on a property investment and lost. But he still blamed Harry for his financial problems.

Rose clicked her pen, how could a thriving business be stripped of its assets, go from profit to loss without a significant event? Why did William blame Harry for his financial woes? The money hadn't disappeared from the partnership until after William and Donna had resigned and the records showed they both received significant sums when they left the company.

The motion of the train, concentration on the complex relationships and the late hour lulled Rose to sleep. The tannoy woke her as the train pulled into Edinburgh Waverley. She stretched and shook herself trying to unscramble the blur of images that recurred while she slept, why on earth did she keep dreaming about horse drawn carriages? But any sense that could be made was already lost to the morning.

The aroma from a fresh batch of lightly spiced apricot jam filled muffins penetrated her senses as she opened the door to her shop.

"Hey Trixie, I'm back."

"Just in time for coffee and scran, which ye look like ye need Rose." Trixie appeared almost instantly from the back carrying a plate and a steaming mug.

"I'm impressed, were you not plugged into your tunes?"

"Noo, Rob just called, the cash and carry is oot of flour! Ah then I heard yer key in the door."

Rose felt her mood plummet. They could manage to produce their baked goods on a few ingredients, but without flour, they would be sunk. Her slim financial margins didn't allow for purchasing flour at supermarket prices.

Trixie held up her hand, "Dinnae worry Rose, It's OK. They've managed tae get their sister store to give them an emergency supply for regulars. Ah was panicky there too."

Rose sat down at the table in the window. "You two are awesome. Thanks for..." Her words trailed off. The weight of everything she had tried not to feel since leaving Bristol had descended. Her choice to fixate on what had happened to Constance and Harry had enabled her to keep herself together, avoiding the painful reality of what she felt after she left her father.

Trixie leaned over the table and put her hand on Rose's arm. "Och Rose, let it go, the door is locked, we dinnae open fer anither hour. Nay one, especially me, is goin' tae tell ye nay tae greet."

"I'm afraid if I start, I won't know how to stop." She wiped her eyes with her sleeve and took a bite of the muffin. "Delicious Trixie, absolutely perfect."

Trixie beamed. "Thanks. I best get back in the kitchen. What are your plans? Ye mentioned somethin' 'bout heading tae Perth in yer text last night."

Rose nodded. "Can you cope for another day?"

"Ay, o' course. Rose, are ye sure ye should be meddlin' right now? I mean, the trip tae Perth, it's about Constance, the woman who died. Am Ah right?"

"Yes."

"Are ye sure it wasnae jist a horrible accident? Would'nae your pal Anthony tell ye tae wind in yer heed?"

Rose spluttered into her coffee, laughing. Trixie was the best medicine ever.

"Maybe, he would, but not quite like that. Maybe it was just an accident, but I've found some financial issues. Why would her friend Harry take his own life so soon after she was found? There are just things that don't add up."

"An' thinking aboot that means ye don't have tae think aboot yer Faither?"

Rose nodded. "You know me well, Trixie. And yes, in part, you're right." Rose wanted to tell Trixie the other reason, about what was happening to her sight. But she stopped herself.

Trixie shrugged. She knew there was little point in saying anything more. She could see Rose's mind was made up.

"I should be back later. I'll come in to do some prep, ready for tomorrow. Will you be alright until Rob gets here? I need to drop my stuff off at my flat, and change, but I can stay if you need me." Rose was aware that she was putting Trixie between a rock and a hard place, the employer asking her employee for permission to do something she would do anyway.

"Away ye go Rose. Just please be careful."

"I will, don't worry. Look, it's a puzzle, I want to put the pieces together. That's all."

As soon as she was back in her flat, Rose put in a call to Donna Meikle to arrange a time to meet.

"You're the woman who met William in London?"

"Yes. I guessed he would have told you we met. I also met his ex wife Andrea. I thought it would be easier to talk in person than over the phone. I really liked Constance. It was Harry who introduced us."

"I don't know what more I can tell you, I mean Constance's death was an accident and Harry killed himself. I have no idea why. If you can be here by three, I have time to meet this afternoon. After that I'm booked for the evening and tomorrow I'm going down to London to visit William."

"There's a train from Haymarket that will get me to Perth at quarter to three. Shall I come to Scone, or would you prefer to meet in Perth?"

"There's a coffee shop on Bridge Street, Beans, it's easy enough to find or you can get a taxi from Perth station."

Unlike Andrea, Donna, also in her fifties, was in peak health. Her presence in the cafe was commanding. The other customers appeared to recognise her and take notice when she arrived wearing jodhpurs and a smart sweater. Her chestnut hair was caught up in a netted chignon at the back.

"Sorry, no time to change," she said, using an outdoor voice more suited to a farm. She made a point of brushing the covering of the bench chair before she sat at the table with her back to the window, opposite Rose.

"No worries. So you ride as well?"

"My horses are the only thing that keeps me sane these days."

"Is that how you met Constance, through riding?"

"Yes. Didn't Andrea fill you in? I was a PA at the National Horse Charity when she was asked to be a patron."

"Andrea told me you and Constance had been friends."

Donna pursed her lips. "I'm closer to her cousin. I'm godmother to her cousin's oldest daughter, Melissa. Constance didn't really make friends. She preferred horses."

"Right. But Harry was her close friend, I supplied catering to a party he threw for her. That's when she became a customer."

Donna frowned. "Look, what is this really all about? According to William, you didn't really even know Constance or Harry, apart from as customers who ordered from your shop."

"He's right. I just ... well ... don't you think it was odd that she said she was going out to Canada. It bothers me and I can't bear an unsolved puzzle? By the way, is this you in Canada with Constance's cousin and their family?" Rose brought up the picture Mike had sent to her on her phone.

Donna glanced at the image, her eyes narrowed as she recognised herself. "Where on earth did you get that?"

"It's online, a friend found it. It's odd it came up, because neither you or William have any online presence. Which one is your goddaughter?"

"The oldest, I told you. Look, Constance was complicated. Her relationship with her cousin was too. I can't say any more. Despite her death, a promise is a promise."

"What do you mean?"

"This was a mistake. I have to go. If I were you I'd forget all about Constance Brown and Harry Turnbull. Live your life. Bye Rose."

Donna pushed the table back and marched out of the cafe without looking back. Rose got up to follow her, to apologise for whatever she had said to offend, but by the time she reached the door Donna was already reversing the Land Rover out of the parking space.

Rose looked at the picture again. What was it about this picture that had upset Donna? And what did she mean about a secret? Rose looked at the photograph again. She wished she had asked the names of the other children, it probably wasn't important but she liked to have names when she connected people in her maps, however tenuously they were connected in real life.

She decided to walk through the park towards the station; she had over an hour to wait for the next train back to Edinburgh. It was as she was crossing Bridge Street towards the park she glanced back and noticed a younger man walking behind her, she remembered seeing him on the train coming up to Perth. Two streets later she stopped in the doorway of a shop and looked at the reflection in the glass, he was still there. Rose stopped, pulled out her phone and pretended to check herself. She reversed the lens, to try and capture his image, but whoever he was he had disappeared. She shook herself and muttered, "stop it" under her breath.

The Edinburgh Fringe murder case was solved, but the well connected perpetrator was still at large. She was mindful of the threats that had been made towards her and Anthony, and the young man had unsettled her. She didn't fancy taking the secluded walk alone now and walked back through the town towards the station.

She looked around the waiting room. There were only three other passengers in there, a couple sharing a sandwich and a casually dressed woman in her twenties. The young woman was texting rapidly, then sat motionless, staring intensely at her phone. Rose assumed she was waiting for a reply. They all three boarded the train as it arrived, choosing separate carriages. As the train pulled out from the station she saw the man she had thought was following her earlier standing on the platform opposite. Rose sighed, relieved and laughing at herself and her moment of panic. He was travelling further North so clearly he wasn't following her.

Rose decided she needed to go to a support meeting before going to the shop and starting on the prep. She was chasing shadows and her imagination had gone into overdrive. She took a walk afterwards, the evening air helped clear her head and relieve the tension she had been holding in her body. But the release was short-lived.

Chapter 6

Rose was checking her phone before bed when she saw the headlines. River Tay Tragedy. Women drowned in Land Rover crash. She clicked on the story. No name had been given for the driver, but according to the bulletin the crash had happened in the early evening, almost three hours after Rose had caught the train. The Land Rover had been seen driving recklessly, before swerving and ending up in the River on the other side of the bridge. Her stomach churned, convinced it was Donna, Rose sent a text to Anthony.

Hey, I think the woman I met earlier today in Perth has been involved in a crash. Any old police mates up in that direction?

She pulled out her notebook. Constance, Harry and now Donna, if it was Donna, all dead within the space of three months of each other. Did that mean William was in danger too, or had she read him wrong?

Her phone started chirping, it was Anthony.

"You're still up, thanks for calling."

"Ha ha Rose, this old dog isn't quite ready for Horlicks and slippers by nine o' clock. What's all this about in Perth? Who did you meet?"

"Donna Meikle. She was a friend of Constance Brown and Harry Turnbull, well they were former business partners. She was driving a Land Rover when I met her today. A woman in a Land Rover went into the Tay. She's dead, but they haven't released her name."

"Ah, Constance Brown. You're still thinking about her?"

"Yes. Look, I know Constance's death looked like an accident, but, if it was Donna who was in the Land Rover, that's three people who knew each other, had all been business partners, dead within three months of each other. And there's another thing. Their business was doing really well, but millions either vanished or were somehow re-directed, when I looked at the records on Companies House."

"Slow down Rose. There could be lots of reasons for that. Maybe they moved the money into another company, an offshore account for tax reasons. You don't know for sure that it was Donna Meikle who died today"

"No. I was hoping you could find out."

"Rose. After what happened to you both times you have got yourself involved with police work, haven't you had enough?"

"I really want to know what happened to Constance, this isn't like before."

"How is it different?"

"Anthony, please don't scold me"

"I'm not meaning to and I don't have any old police mates as you call them in Perth, but there is a woman who has just joined Edinburgh as an inspector from Perth. Her name is Hickson. I know her a bit. But I can't call her at this hour."

"Would they have told her brother, do you think? I met him when I was in London."

"If he is her next of kin, yes, probably. He would be asked to identify her. Isn't there anyone geographically closer?"

"No. Donna was a widow."

"Look Rose, you can't go calling up a relative and ask if they have just been told a family member is dead. What if it isn't her?"

"I really think it is. More than think, I'm pretty sure actually."

"And what do you think her death means, Rose?"

"I think someone is killing them off, one by one, making it look like an accident. William, the brother might be next. I've no idea who or why, except I have a feeling it has something to do with the money that's missing."

"As you don't know any money is missing, your hypothesis doesn't hold water. It's all conjecture. Sorry to be such a stickler for detail, but where's the evidence?"

"Right. You're right." Rose sighed into her phone.

"I'm not saying there isn't something in what you're thinking. I just don't want you to light a fire and find it's out of control. The best I can do is suggest you get a good night's sleep, and I'll promise to phone Hickson first thing. Will that do?"

"Thanks Anthony, it's just ..., you know."

Anthony let out a laugh. "Yes Rose, indeed I do. Your gut. Now let's both get some sleep. I'll call you tomorrow."

"Night. Thanks."

But Rose did not have a good night. The disturbing dream she'd had following her birthday dinner returned. This time Troy's face was unmasked and there was another man. Rose was locked in a horse drawn carriage and made to watch as they both shot at the horses Troy's laughter echoing through the night air as the four beasts fell to the ground. Suddenly her mother appeared, walking towards the carriage. Troy raised his gun directly at her mother's face and fired. She woke up screaming 'stop' several times over.

Splashing her face with cold water Rose shivered. The dream was getting more vivid. She wanted to drink the memory away. She was about to call her sponsor when her phone pinged with a text from Anthony.

It was Donna Meikle who crashed yesterday. The report I saw on the news said a suspected DUI.

Rose responded, *She was sober as a judge when she left me. She didn't look the type either.*

The path report won't be back yet. 'Type', is there one? She might have been drinking secretly.

I know all the tricks. No, she definitely wasn't drinking.

OK. I'll. Do you want me to give the DI in Perth your contact details, see if he wants to speak to you? My guess is it would probably be Hickson from Edinburgh you'll hear from, I doubt Perth will send someone down.

Sure, no problem, are you busy later? Fancy indulging me?

How?

To see where Constance lived. Take a look, talk to a neighbour.

No Rose. Sorry. Isn't Rob usually your go to assistant sleuth?

Yeah, but without all your experience! Sorry, I didn't mean to put you in an awkward spot.

OK, I suppose it wouldn't do any harm. BUT we have to stay within the law, no breaking and entering. Deal?

Deal. Thanks. I'll need to work at the shop and give Trixie and Rob a break. Around 6?

I'll come over to Morrison just before you close.

Great. I'll have the kettle boiled and save you a muffin.

Ha ha. My expanding retirement waistline will not thank you. See you later, Rose.

The conversation with Anthony had broken the spell the dream held over her, but she recognised the see-saw she was on. She daren't risk chancing the day without support. She sent a text to Trixie.

Morning. I'm going to a meeting. I'll be in by 9 to take over. Do you want to take this afternoon and tomorrow off?'

I'm good. Thanks though, perhaps a couple of days next week? That recipe change you left for the Spring Surprise muffin works well. Shall I do a taster test batch? I've redesigned the topping to resemble a daisy.

Sounds perfect. Thanks Trixie.

"Long time no see," said Rob as Rose arrived. He was sorting out the bike for the second round of deliveries.

"You've been amazing, you and Trixie. We seem to be getting more orders from different cafés. Are you coping with all this extra work?"

"Yeah, it's all good. How about you Rose, are you really okay, with your Dad and everything? Trixie said you went to a meeting this morning."

"Yeah, last night too. It's just Dad and then, well there have been some dreams. Troy was in them."

"Troy? How come?"

"I don't know. Another man appeared in the dream last night. And then ... my mother. Troy aimed a gun at her."

Rob pulled her in and gave her a hug. "Enough. Rose, I'm sorry. That bastard deserved more than the sentence he'll serve."

Rose shook herself away and smiled, "You said it, Rob."

The shop was bustling all day. Trixie's taste tester batch for the revised Spring Surprise had been a hit and they had several orders for the full size muffin. The lemon, honey and cardamom mixture hadn't been popular when they first made them. Rose had adjusted the measurements, changed honey for dark agave syrup and included a hint of vanilla pod. Rob and Trixie were helping clear everything up, preparing for the next day when Anthony arrived at the shop.

"There was a time when I got worried about you walking through that door," laughed Rob, "Tea?"

"I promised him a muffin too," Rose called from the back kitchen.

"Oh, I'm very harmless these days. But your boss isn't. Still poking her fingers into pies that she shouldn't. Thanks for this." Anthony took the mug of tea and plated muffin and sat down at the window table. The same table where he and Rose had first had a conversation about murder.

"Rose, come oan, tell us aboot yon pies." Trixie shouted. "I telt ye tae stop meddling."

Rose looked over at their expectant faces, all gathered at the table with mugs of tea. "You all already know what I think. Constance Brown's death was not an accident. Maybe I would have bought that story if her friend Harry hadn't committed suicide, and now another business partner, Donna Meikle is dead too."

"Whoa, three deaths?" Rob looked shocked. "I didn't realise."

Rose nodded. "I think each death has been cleverly concealed, two accidents and a suicide."

Anthony opened his hands towards her, "You really don't know or do you have any evidence for saying that."

"I do," she pointed to her stomach, "In here."

Trixie looked across at Anthony. "Ah hate to say it but, she's nae been wrang up tae noo. Her gut an' yon maps she makes."

"Which is why I am here. We're going to see where Constance lived."

"Och Rose, whit aboot Rob? Rob you've been superseded. How ye feelin'?" Trixie gave a deep chuckle.

Rob held up his hands. "Oh I'm well out of it, after last time, nearly getting my pants burned off."

Rose grinned at the good humoured banter. She knew they all had her back. She wasn't going to put Rob or Trixie at risk again. At least Anthony had once been a policeman.

It was a dry bright evening. The half hour walk to Morningside took them past The Meadows where Rose had lived before moving to Corstorphine. The sun was behind them, casting a long shadow ahead of each of them on the pavement.

"This is it," Anthony pointed to the large semi detached sand coloured stone building that had once been a house. Some of the houses in the street were still semi detached individual family homes, others, like the one Constance had lived in had been divided into flats. Constance's apartment was on the middle floor, facing onto the street.

Rose pulled out her phone and was about to take a picture of the building when a young woman with a child in a buggy came out of the front door.

"You going to be our new neighbour?" She spoke with an eastern European accent. She was fair skinned and wore a hat pulled low over her face. The child who was about two years old was busy with a sippy cup.

"Is the flat for rent already? I used to know the woman who lived here."

"The one who died?"

"Yes, did you know her?"

"Not really. She didn't ever speak to anyone. Especially not someone like me."

"What do you mean?"

The young woman shrugged. "My daughter is good, but when she was a baby she had colic. I did my best, but I think the crying annoyed her. I would see her at the window, staring down into the street. The way she looked at me was creepy, especially when she changed her hair."

"What do you mean?"

"Well she had nice hair before, blonde, but then she dyed it brown. It didn't suit her , made her look older."

" I see. Well, I didn't ever meet her, face to face, she was a customer. She was nice on the phone. You didn't think anything of it when you hadn't seen her at the window for a while?"

"Yes, we did, we even reported it to the landlord, asked him to go into the flat because of the smell, but he didn't. When we first moved in, before the baby, we knocked to introduce ourselves, gave her a Christmas card, but she didn't respond. Then, after last Christmas we saw the mail pile up. The smell, it was everywhere. We live above. It started to permeate the whole flat. It was the postie who made the police take notice. By the time they found out what had happened, we were ready to move out. But it's hard finding somewhere around here."

"Your landlord didn't do anything?"

"The agents gave me scented plug-ins and suggested we keep the windows open!"

"Did she speak to anyone else in the building, do you know?"

"I don't think so. I think we all hoped she had gone somewhere else. I don't mean we hoped she was dead, but honestly, I didn't lose any sleep wondering what had happened to her. Look, I need to go, or I'll be getting this little missy out of her routine. I stupidly forgot milk earlier."

"Oh, of course. Thanks for your time." Rose looked at Anthony and raised her eyebrows. "Well that puts a different light on things I suppose. Not that I don't still think her death is suspicious, just that I had a very different perspective about what Constance was like. She was formal, but always polite and friendly on the phone. Why didn't she speak to her neighbours I wonder?"

Anthony nodded, "There's something else. I know Morningside is expensive, but I'm surprised by her choice of accommodation. I had the impression she was very wealthy."

Rose looked at the building and tipped her head to one side. "One of these flats would set you back quite a bit to buy, and I expect they're huge inside. Unless ...-"

"Unless what?"

"Unless she owned the building? The company dealt in paper, but according to a woman I met in London, they had a portfolio of property too."

"Doesn't explain why there was a landlord for the flat above." Anthony observed.

"She used the word agent, I said landlord. I may be barking up the wrong tree, but ...-" Rose broke off and smiled as she saw Anthony pointing to her stomach

"It's a gut feeling?"

"Yep. Shall we see if anyone else is home?"

"You go ahead Rose." He nodded towards a board advertising a flat for rent in the adjoining building. I'll call the agents and see if I can find out anything about the owner, or owners."

"Well if she did own both sides, it's worth a pretty big chunk of money, especially if she bought them years ago."

"Remember our deal, no illegal entering ...?"

"Got it."

Rose headed up the path and started to press the other flat intercoms one by one. It looked as if there were two flats on the ground floor, two on the upper floor and one on the middle floor, which was where Constance had lived.

Rose crossed the path to the adjoining house, there were six flats, with the middle floor divided.

She went back to join Anthony. There was no answer from any of the intercoms. Either everyone was out or they weren't interested in answering the door to unexpected callers. He held up his finger as she approached and nodded, clicking his phone off.

"I have a feeling your gut was right."

"Both sides are owned by a corporation. They have managed the lettings for over twenty years. But this month, they were given notice."

"Did they say why or give you a name?"

"No. I was speaking to the receptionist but the manager overheard. I heard him stop her from giving me more information. She put me through to speak to him, but he was very guarded."

Rose made a face, wishing she had spoken to the agents instead. Anthony's background as a policeman was making him too cautious.

He watched her pull a face. "You think you would have persuaded him, don't you Rose?"

"Maybe. Sorry I didn't intend to be mean."

"I know. But charging in with all guns sometimes doesn't get the results. If you'd let me finish I was going to say that I have arranged to go to meet him for a pint. He was just closing the office. Thursday is their late night."

Rose rolled her eyes and put two fingers to her head. "That'll teach me."

Anthony smiled. "Do you want to come?"

"No, you go. I think I'll hang about here and see if I can speak to any of the other tenants, one of them must have noticed something."

"Right. But the police will have spoken to them."

"But if they thought Constance's death was an accident, they wouldn't be looking for anything to suggest otherwise."

"True."

"Did you get a call from Inspector Hickson by the way?"

"Yes. She's coming to talk to me tomorrow."

"I've only met her a couple of times. I think you'll like her. I'll let you know if I find anything else out from meeting the manager."

"OK, and thanks for coming with me."

Rose had been standing outside the building on the pavement for about ten minutes when she heard a tap on the window from the ground floor flat. She looked up and saw an older woman standing in the window, she was holding the lace curtain to one side. She opened the window slightly, then beckoned to Rose. "Who are you? Are you with the new people who are taking over the building?"

"No, I knew the woman who died. My name's Rose McLaren, I used to send gifts on her behalf from my shop. I was hoping to talk to someone who knew her."

"I did, a bit. Do you want to come in? Flat one, just inside to the right of the stairs."

"Are you sure?"

The woman nodded. " You look safe enough to me," she said as she fastened the window.

"Thank you for letting me in. How long have you lived here?" Rose had been right about the flats being spacious. This one high ceilinged, bright and airy, with lots of character and lots of original features. Whoever had done the conversion had done it well.

"Oooh, since the flats were first done, about fifteen years. I needed somewhere smaller once my husband passed, closer to my daughter."

"It is lovely."

"Yes, but now, with the new rent, I may have to move."

"New rent?"

"We all had letters about a week back. The new owners are doing an upgrade and we have a choice to sign or not. But as I say ..." Her voice trailed off and she looked down, blinking her eyes quickly.

"That's too bad. Have you spoken to the Citizens advice bureau? You daughter, has she made inquiries?"

"There's nothing that can be done. Everything they are doing they have a right to do apparently."

"Do you want to show me the letter? My friend, the man I was with, is away to talk to the old agents."

"I'd better check with my daughter. You said you wanted to talk about the woman who died. Mrs Brown?"

"Yes. I was very upset to read about what happened to her. You knew her a bit?"

"As a neighbour. She wasn't very social, but she'd always say hello. Then there was a huge row one day, and then that accident with the horse, you know, the one that was in all the papers. After that I stopped seeing her going in and out. We had press here for days after the poor horse was shot."

"That must have been upsetting. And do you mean she didn't go out after the accident, or just that she avoided seeing anyone?"

"I can't be sure, but I don't think she went out after that happened. Her friend came though, usually early in the evening, for about an hour. Then he'd slip away."

Rose was intrigued by her description, slipping away. "Can you tell me why you said that, that he slipped away I mean."

The woman made a face. "He had a key right enough, but he always made sure the door closed without a sound, coming and going. I only realised he was in and out because I keep that one curtain open, until I'm away to bed. The lace panel means I can still see out, but no-one can see in. I'm not spying on my neighbours, but I feel safer if I know who's in and out, if you know what I mean. Everyone else just lets the door close automatically, there's a definite sound."

Rose nodded. "Isn't that annoying?"

"No, I'm used to it. It's comforting in an odd way. Less lonely."

Rose changed tack, she wasn't feeling up to engaging in whatever personal tragedy had befallen her. "What did her friend look like? Was this the man by any chance?" Rose pulled up a picture of Harry Turnbull on her phone.

"Yes, that's him. Before she stopped going out, I would see them going off together, all very dressed up too, some of the time."

"You mentioned a row. Was that with her friend?"

"No, although he was there, he was the one who saw them off. A young couple, mid twenties, maybe a bit older."

"Had you seen them before? Can you describe them?"

"No, sorry. I don't think I had seen them before and it's too long ago, I can't remember what they looked like. A man and a woman, American I think, from the man's voice. Yes, definitely American."

The woman's telephone began to ring. It was an old fashioned model, plugged into the wall. "That'll be my daughter. She always calls about now."

"Better get it, or she'll worry. Thanks. Mind if I pop back and see if she thinks it is ok for me to see the letter?"

"Hold on, I'll ask her now. Janice, is that you. Yes dear, I'm fine. I have a guest. She used to send gifts for Mrs Brown, from upstairs. You know, the one who fell and died. She wants to see the letter about the rent. Is that alright do you think?" She held the mouthpiece of the phone out to Rose. "Janice wants to speak to you."

Rose explained who she was, and why she was there. Janice agreed that she could see the letter, although she couldn't see what good it could do. They had explored every angle. The flats were changing hands and the new owners, 'foreigners', could do as they wished, through some gap in the law.

"That's too bad, and you're right I'm not sure how I can help. Your mum has such a nice place. It will be awful for her if she loses it." Rose handed the phone back to the old woman. "I'll make a copy of the letter on my phone and I'll be in touch if I think of anything."

"Thank you hen, but I think I'm resigned to having to move now." She said, as she handed Rose a thick manilla envelope. There was no postmark, but the name and return address of the sender was stamped on the back. A firm of lawyers based in London.

Chapter 7

Rose had arranged to meet Inspector Hickson at the shop before they opened. The woman was younger than she had expected, at the beginning of her career, but moving up the ranks quickly. Her unmade-up fresh complexion and clear green eyes spoke to Rose of clean living and a strict fitness regime, a stark contrast to the chubby and ruddy faced DCI Chatterton. Although Anthony had slimmed down a lot since he had retired, he would never again have the bright eyes of this young successor.

"Coffee or tea?" asked Rose as the woman removed her jacket and pulled out her notebook.

"Just water thanks. Tap is fine."

Trixie wrinkled her nose and grinned as Rose gave an eye roll and mouthed 'tap water' at her silently, pulling a face.

"Ah'll fetch 'em, just a tick," said Trixie.

"So, this is the famous muffin shop that the station staff support. Business doing well?"

"Yes, I'm lucky, we're popular with locals and regulars. Your lot from the station has been great too. It's not as if we're that local. We often supply boxes of biscuits and muffins for big meetings."

Hickson gave a curt smile and tapped her pen on her notebook. "So, to business, how did you know Donna Meikle?"

"I didn't really. She was a friend of Constance Brown, who was a customer before she died. I went to meet her because …" Rose looked down. She had no idea if Anthony had told the inspector about Rose's suspicions regarding Constance's death. And even to her own ears, preparing to say it out loud and out of context, sounded mad.

"Because?"

"How much do you know about me?" Rose said finally.

"Nothing at all. What should I know?"

"I helped DCI Chatterton a couple of times, solving murders I mean. I spoke to him because, well to be honest, Constance Brown, the woman who was found dead just before Easter … I don't think her death was an accident."

Inspector Hickson gazed at Rose without expression. Her affect was calm as she took a sip of water. "I see. So you regard yourself as something of a detective Rose. Is that right? What are your qualifications?"

"No, no not at all. It's just that I am good at reading people, putting things together, puzzles if you like. Her death, the way Constance was found and the fact she lied about travelling to Canada, it just doesn't seem right. Then Harry Turnbull, her business partner and lifelong friend, commits suicide. Now Donna Meikle has died in a car accident. All within three months of each other.

"Accidents, suicides and preventable deaths happen all the time Rose. Otherwise the crime statistics would soar and half the population would be banged up for murder, according to your theory. Donna Meikle was either high or drunk or both. That is why she crashed. What I want to know from you is why you have told the former DCI that she couldn't have been incapacitated and why you were meeting her?"

"I'm an alcoholic. I can read people when they have been drinking secretly. I know the signs. Donna was sober when she left me in the cafe and to be honest she didn't look like a drinker. It's like Constance, the way it happened, it doesn't make sense, I mean how many cars of that size just veer off the road like that?"

"Maybe you said something to upset her? Made her need to get a drink. Did you Rose? What did you talk to her about? Maybe you know your way around narcotics too?"

Rose decided to ignore the reference to drugs. She sensed the Inspector was fishing and she wasn't about to give her anything that she could turn against her. That was a lesson learned long ago. "I talked to her about Constance. I also showed her a picture from my phone. The picture was of her and her cousin in Canada. It seemed to upset her somehow. Do you want to see it?"

"Yes."

Rose turned on her phone and turned it round for the inspector to view. The images of the envelope and documents she had taken from the flat the night before came up first.

"What are those? The address on that envelope is the same as Constance Brown. Why do you have a picture of that?"

"You have sharp eyes Inspector. The flats where Constance Brown lived are being sold. I met a downstairs neighbour. I said I would look into seeing if I could think of anything that might help her not have to move. This is the photograph I showed to Donna."

Inspector Hickson looked at the image, her expression gave nothing away. Rose was clueless whether the photograph meant anything to her, or if she had seen it before. But then she wasn't based in Perth, and would not have had access to Donna's personal effects.

"Can you send me a copy of the photo to this email?" She took a card out of a tiny black shoulder bag. The minimalist structure of the bag mirrored the cold efficiency of its owner.

"Sure. Is there anything else?"

"Not for now Rose. But I suggest you focus on your business from now on and leave me to do the police work I am paid to do. If you plan to go anywhere, please let me know about it first."

Rose felt herself irked by the request, but she remained outwardly calm. "OK, sure. No trips planned for now apart from to see my father. He lives in Bristol."

"That's alright then. Bye Rose." She stood up and turned to leave. The bell jangled as she closed the door. Rose remained seated, watching the woman stride further up Morrison Street.

"Well, yon lassie's a bit o' a cold fish, nae like Anthony at a'," said Trixie coming over to the table with a mug of hot coffee. "Ye want another Rose?"

"No, thanks Trixie," Rose sighed. The interview had been awkward. Trixie was right, the woman had been cold and formal from the outset. Rose suspected she knew more about Rose and her history than she had let on.

"Anthony thought she and I would get on. But it seems not. I'll send her the picture and hope I don't have anything more to do with her."

"Wha' aboot Constance and the man who killed himself, Harry. Are ye nay goin' tae bother? Ah mean, ye know Ah would be glad if ye didnae do ony more poking an' prying."

"You know what Trixie, I'm going to leave it well alone. Except for the poor woman in the flats Constance owned. I am going to try and help her. If I can. I want to pop down and see Dad at the weekend, if that's OK with you, I can stop off in London on Monday, to see these solicitors and come back on a late train or the sleeper. I'll let her daughter know, then give them a call to set up an appointment.

"Ay Rose, fill yer boots wi' the legal eagles and stay awa' from murderers," Trixie laughed.

But when Rose called the London number the brusque woman on the other end of the call told her that Mr Mathers, the solicitor handling the property, was not available. She left her name anyway and asked for someone to call her back. Then she remembered something that Andrea Summers had said. She checked the name of the lawyers against the notes she had made after talking with Andrea. "Rooney and Mathers" she said aloud. "Mathers, I am sure that's the same name."

Chapter 8

Rose arrived in Bristol just after 7pm the following Friday. It was too late to visit her father and she had arranged to meet Kay Sandeep for dinner. They had spoken two or three times since her last visit to Bristol and she was looking forward to seeing the woman again. Kay was at the station waiting for her.

"This is kind, to meet me here I mean. Where do you want to go for dinner, my treat."

Kay smiled and shook her head. "No actually, it's mine. I've made dinner at my place. I hope that's OK."

"Really? Even better, I love home cooked food and it's been a long day travelling."

"That's what I thought. You can wash and rest up while I finish off the cooking. You could even stay if you want. I have a spare bedroom."

"Wow, talk about feeling spoiled. I may just take you up on that. I didn't fancy the hotel I stayed at in town before, I was going to look for a B & B out near the care home once I was here."

"No need. Stay with me. I meant to say that on the phone, but our calls always seemed to get interrupted with your work or my pager. I'm on call from tomorrow. If I get called out, feel free to just make yourself at home. There's tons of food and books."

Kay's apartment was on the second floor of a Georgian terrace in Clifton, on the west side of Bristol city centre. The floors were bare wood stripped and covered in various rugs of contrasting colours. Kay had painted the walls in shades of soft ochre, with a bold red covering the wall behind the fireplace in the living room. The kitchen reminded Rose of the Mediterranean, with yellow ochre walls and Aegean blue cupboard doors. "You have amazing taste, Kay. It's beautiful."

Kay smiled, "Thanks. I love colour, vanilla doesn't suit me at all. Your bedroom is a bit bold I'm afraid," she said, opening the door to a willow and sage green interior. An old fashioned brass bed stood against the middle wall, covered in a bright yellow, pink and red quilt. The bedside lamps boasted enormous maroon shades with painted red dragonflies. One wall was completely covered with wall to floor bookcases, full of books.

Rose gasped. "I love it, it's so different from my bedroom. I'm a bit grey and vanilla when it comes to decorating."

Kay patted her on the shoulder, "Bathroom is just across the hall. There are towels in the chest at the bottom of the bed. Make yourself comfy, I'll be in the kitchen. Chai or coffee?"

"Chai, please." Rose sat on the bed and looked around her. Kay had been right about books, there must be four hundred in this room alone. She had noticed bookshelves in the living room and there were more in the hallway. She lay back on the bed and looked up at the crystal chandelier. The glass was catching the light from the sun sending patterns across her hands as she held them up. It was the first time in months she had felt completely relaxed. Giving up trying to work out what had happened to Constance had been a smart choice. She had even torn up her notes and pulled the beginnings of a new map out of her notebook. The dreams had stopped too. No more horses were being shot at and Troy hadn't tried to steal his way into her mind at all.

Rose showered and came back to find a steaming mug of chai on the bedside table. Kay had put on some music, Rose swayed to the jazz bossa nova in front of the long mirror as she combed her short hair and gave her body the once over. Despite the messed up years, drinking, street life and drugs, she looked fit.

Dressed in a fresh shirt and leggings she made her way to the kitchen. Kay was ladling three different vegetable curries onto two plates. "I hope you're OK with naan bread instead of rice. I think it mops up the juices better. Here, take a seat, it's all ready." She pointed to a pine table in the corner of the kitchen.

"That was amazing," said Rose, patting her stomach, leaning back against the cushioned banquette as she and Kay downed their forks on the now empty plates at the same time.

"Thanks, it's good to have someone to cook for. I do sometimes have friends over, but for the last year I haven't bothered so much, since ..." She broke off and looked down. A tear had formed in the corner of her eye.

"Hey, what's up?"

"Oh, ignore me," Kay brushed the tear with her finger and attempted a smile. Rose could see she was trying to fake a recovery from whatever had upset her.

"I don't want to push you to talk about it, whatever it is, but I'm a good listener if you want or need to."

"Thanks, but I should get over myself. No point dwelling on the past and what if's, is there?" Kay started to get up and sort the dishes.

"Why don't I do that, after all you have just cooked." Rose reached across the table, took the two plates from Kay and went over to the sink. Kay had sunk back down onto the banquette. Rose sensed what Kay was feeling, she knew it all too well. One minute you were in the moment and everything was fine when suddenly a ghost rises up to snatch away the well-being. "Do you need to be alone Kay?"

"No, but thanks for asking. I think I've been alone too much recently."

"Having me here reminded you of when you weren't alone?"

"My, you are astute Rose, yes. I was in a relationship for two years, until just before Halloween last year."

"Was he a doctor?"

"She. No, that was part of the problem, my hours, being on call and my family. They didn't know about her, and still don't. The fact that I refused to marry when they had it all arranged, to find out that I prefer women, well, they would never speak to me again. She worked in public relations, she wanted to travel, and party. We just grew further and further apart."

"It doesn't make it any less painful though, even when you know it's not going to work out."

"No, you're right. It doesn't. She was my first big love. Sorry, I didn't mean to do this, you have a lot going on with your Dad and the puzzle you were trying to solve. You don't need to hear about my stupid love life, or lack of it."

"Oh Kay, your love life sounds like it has been much less stupid than mine. So why don't you tell me all about her, while I clean up and make us both something hot to drink."

Snuggled under blankets on the two comfy couches in the living room Kay told Rose about her past lover and the familial complications facing her as a gay Asian woman. Rose shared some of her own life story, about Troy and how she had ended up in prison.

"So I think I win on the stupid category, but complicated, Kay you definitely win the prize for that category. I had no idea."

Kay grinned, "It's sad and ironic at the same time. My family desperately wants me to be married, but if I told them I wanted to marry a woman, I would be dead to them, and as it is I hardly see them now."

Later, Rose climbed into bed and pulled the colourful blanket around her. Talking to Kay was cathartic. They had laughed long and hard about past choices, things that Rose would never have dreamed she could laugh about. By saying them out loud, she had been able to release some of the tension, recognise the fears haunting her; that she would somehow end up back on the streets, or worse, back in prison. She held onto Kay's words as she closed her eyes and drifted to sleep in the comfortable brass bed. "Troy can't hurt you now Rose, he has no power over you."

Rose spent most of the following day at the care home. Her father was in and out of sleep. When he was awake he was confused about who she was one minute, then briefly remembering the next. She organised a chair to take him for a walk in the grounds in the afternoon. He came alive outside, pointing at plants and trees and telling her their names.

"I planted those roses for your mum Rose, do you remember," he said suddenly lucid, knowing who she was. Rose knelt down and pulled one of the roses closer towards her to smell it.

"It's lovely Dad. Yellow roses were mum's favourite."

"Where is your mother, she was supposed to be back for lunch."

Rose knew from what the carers had told her that her father slipped in and out of long term and short term memory. That reminding him his wife was dead was not helpful. But when she tried to distract him with another topic his old watery eyes stared back at her vacantly. Rose read to him, sat with him and did all the things a dutiful daughter who had once had a close relationship with her father might have done. However hard she wished that closeness had never been true. If it hadn't been for the letter he had written to her, she knew it would have been almost impossible to do what she was doing now. But at the end of his life, and to honour the memory of her mother, It seemed little enough to ask of herself.

Rose was on her way back to Kay's flat when the text pinged in from Kay.

Sorry Rose. I'm having to go in. Probably won't be back until the early hours.

Understanding, but disappointed, Rose turned back towards the town centre. She had been looking forward to getting to know more about her new friend. The day with her father had been tiring. She was about to cross a busy intersection when a car horn made her jump. The man inside the car was waving at her and gesturing for her to wait for him on the other side of the road. It was Alan Pearson, her father's solicitor.

"Hello Miss McLaren. I'm glad I caught you. I've just been to the care home. I need some signatures from you." He was dishevelled and reminded Rose of an undisciplined puppy, eager to please.

"Please, call me Rose, you're working on a Saturday?"

He swiped his hand across the air in front of his face. "Just playing catch up. I had meant to drop these off for you yesterday, but I was in court. By the time we were finished I couldn't get back across town. Do you want to go somewhere for a coffee and I can talk you through the papers?"

"Sure, if you don't mind, although I suppose it's all billable."

"Oh, no, I wasn't trying to …"

Rose held up her hand, "It's OK, you're doing your job and you seem to have gone out of your way. Don't sweat it."

"Rose, your Dad, he is a client, but I like him. I'm not one of those legal types, you know the ones who …"

Rose interrupted him again, she felt bad that he had taken her so literally, "I do. In fact, I may have a question for you about the legitimacy of a law firm I'm trying to get in touch with. Shall we settle in over there?" Rose pointed to an Italian coffee shop with tables outside. The windows displaying an assortment of dried meats, cheese, biscotti, panettone and glass jars filled with dried pasta.

They found a table at the back. Rose ordered coffee and pastries for them both. "I hope you don't mind, but I'm starving. The care home food is not all that appetising."

"Not at all. Here are the papers. Do you remember the last time we met, I told you about a trust? You may be surprised when you read what's on that first sheet."

Rose looked at the bundle he had passed to her and did a double take. Her father's estate was worth well over a million pounds, and the house another five hundred thousand. "How on earth? I don't understand."

"Penny shares apparently. He told me he had a friend who created some sort of travel app. Your Dad had given him some start up money, just a loan. Then when things took off, he received shares in the company. Then the company was bought out by one of the big tech giants. I had no idea of the net worth when he first came to me and said there were investments. He wanted to put them in a trust in your name, before he died. To be honest I tried to talk him out of handing over that amount of money, in case he needed it. But he insisted. There'll be capital gains I am afraid, but because of the way we set up the trust for his care needs and expenses out of the savings he had, I don't think you'll have to pay death duties on what's left over, once that day comes."

"I don't know what to say. I'm worth over a million pounds?"

"Yes Rose. You are."

Rose took a gulp of the coffee. "Gobsmacked," she muttered under her breath. "Gobsmacked."

"Totally, congratulations. It's up to you how you want to proceed from here on. The money is available for you immediately according to the instructions he gave me if he became incapacitated. Do you have a financial adviser?"

"Heck no. But now I guess I should find one. Do you know anyone?"

"I can't officially recommend, but I can give you a couple of firms here. You might be better off having someone closer to where you live though."

"True. Who knew that having a windfall like this had its own complications?"

"So what's the name of the law firm you wanted to ask me about?"

"Right. Umm Mather, no Rooney and Mathers, they're based in London and handling a property deal in Edinburgh. The tenants are being kicked out or asked to pay much higher rents by the new owners. I just wanted to see if there was a way around it, so the tenants could keep their homes I mean. I have a copy of the letter they sent out on here, with the new offer and leases."

Rose handed him her phone.

Alan Pearson studied the documents carefully and made a few notes on the table napkin. He sniffed and looked up. "I don't know too much about this side of things but from what they've laid out, it looks legitimate. Here are a couple of questions you might want to ask though." He handed Rose the table napkin.

"Thank you. I guessed it was a long shot, but you never know right?" Rose shrugged her shoulders.

"It's always good to ask, and now I'm afraid I have to leave you and go pick up my kids."

"You have kids?" Rose was surprised, she had pegged Alan Pearson as a hard working bachelor without family ties.

"Yeah, for my sins. Twins! A girl and a boy, both twelve, going on twenty."

"Have fun, and thank you for everything you're doing and have done for my father and me. I'll be in touch. I should probably let my solicitor look over everything before I make any decisions."

"Yes Rose, you should definitely do that. I'm sorry, didn't realise you had one, or I would have dealt directly with them."

"I don't really, just someone local who I know." Rose thought back to Mr Walker who had represented her when she was first charged. He would be surprised if she came to him as a non legal aid client. "I think now I am a woman of means I should have one though, unless you …"

"I could do that Rose, as a family solicitor, but again, someone closer to where you live would probably be easier for you to deal with."

Rose toyed with the remains of her pastry and coffee when her phone pinged. It was Rob.

Have you heard from Sally?

Sally was the student Rose had hired to run the Muffin trailer at the Grassmarket every weekend.

No. Why?

Just been over to see what she needed for tomorrow. But the stall's closed.

Weird. Unlike Sally not to say if something was wrong. Have you tried calling?

Yes. No reply.

OK. I'll try her. If she's sick we can just leave the stall closed tomorrow.

We've baked stuff to sell.

Bag those and freeze them. We can sell them as day old's on Tuesday when we re-open. Just texted Sally now.

You OK? Your Dad?

I'm really good. I'll tell you everything when I'm back. Dinner Tuesday night?

Yeah.

Great, ask Trixie too. I have some good news :-)!

About time!!! Hahaha :-)

Rose checked her phone. Sally hadn't replied, but if she was sick she may have switched her phone off. It seemed odd behaviour for her to just lock up and not check in with anyone, she was usually so reliable.

Trixie, can you access the shop records from your computer? We have another number on file for Sally. An emergency contact.

I called that number when Rob told me Sally had gone. Her mum hasn't heard from her. She was going to contact one of Sal's flatmates and get back to me.

OK, good work. Thanks. Let's hope one of us hears from Sally soon.

Be good to get the float from today back too.

She's probably taken it home for safe keeping. See you Tuesday.

Yeah, Rob said you had good news. Can't wait to hear! :-)

The coffee shop staff were beginning to clear away the debris from the tables and pack up the counters ready to close. Rose made her way back into the street and looked around at the city where she had grown up. It had changed a lot since she was young and she had gone with her mum for shopping trips together. "Ah mum," she whispered aloud. "How I miss you."

Kay was still not back when Rose set out for the care home on Sunday morning. She made a stack of pancakes, baked some muffins to take to the care home and stocked up Kay's cupboards with the groceries she had bought on her way home the previous evening.

Her father was sleeping when she arrived and the staff told her he had had a bad night. They didn't know whether or not he would be able to get up today. She felt guilty, she realised from the staff that her visit on the Saturday had exhausted him. They were kind and told her it was just the way it was. Some days were good, but most of them were like this.

Rose took a walk around the grounds. She wondered if picking one of the roses he had commented on yesterday would stimulate him, lift his spirits. She leaned in to smell them again. The flowers were early. The west of England had hit climate records for sun since Easter. It was only the beginning of May. It felt like a sign somehow, that her mum was watching over them both.

Rose sat by her father for the rest of the afternoon, but he hardly stirred, ate little and didn't know who she was when she tried to help him with the soup.

"Bye dad," she said leaning down, to kiss him on the forehead. He looked very frail. Frailer than yesterday. She reached within, trying to find the peace and sense of well being she had felt after she had talked with Kay, but she felt empty.

Rose pinged a text to Trixie.

Heard anything from Sally?

Trixie reported there was still no news. No-one at her flat, and her mother had called to say they had not heard from her either.

Kay was asleep when she arrived back at the flat. She had left a note for Rose thanking her for the pancakes and said she would probably be awake again by 6. She had put a vegetable casserole in the oven and to help herself if she was hungry before that.

Rose checked the train times for the following morning. She still hadn't heard from Mathers about an appointment. She decided to go straight to his office and then meet up with Andrea Summers at Peter Jones in Sloane Square. Rose had called her on Friday, to ask her what she knew about Mathers. Although she had explained to Andrea she had given up on trying to find out what might have happened to Constance. Andrea had insisted they meet up.

"But not here at the flat, we'll go out. It will be safer."

The connection from the train had cut the conversation off. Rose realised she hadn't thought much more about what Andrea had meant by safer until now. She felt the tension rising in her stomach, the ghosts were back.

Chapter 9

Rose tapped on Kay's door just after 6.30pm. "Hi Kay, you awake, shall I bring you a tray? Your casserole looks and smells delicious."

"Mmm, sorry, just coming back to life. I'll come out. I'm so exhausted, I slept through the alarm."

Kay was fully dressed when she appeared a few moments later to join Rose at the table in the kitchen. "I need to go back to the hospital. Sorry Rose. Not much of a hostess am I."

"I don't know how you do it. Such long hours."

"You have to really love it, but even then, sometimes it is hard. Especially …"

Rose waited for her to finish the sentence, but Kay looked away. Rose tucked in hungrily to the casserole, allowing Kay to stay lost in her thoughts. They finished eating in companionable silence before Rose spoke. Despite everything else, she was excited about what the solicitor had told her about the trust and wanted to share it. She knew Kay would be pleased for her.

"I have some news. I ran into my father's solicitor yesterday. Apparently, he'd set up a trust and gifted me a small fortune. I'd no idea he'd made so much money. You know we weren't close, but now I know he did care about me, it's made a difference, not just the money I mean."

Kay blinked, then smiled faintly. "How nice for you. I imagine the inheritance will be a relief."

"What do you mean a relief?"

Kay looked down. "Nothing. I'm really happy for you Rose."

Rose blinked, the words stung and Kay seemed detached. She watched Kay push the remains of her food to the side of her plate. Without speaking she gathered up the dishes from the table and took them over to the sink.

"Hey, let me do the washing up."

Kay didn't turn around and carried on rinsing the plates under the water. "It's fine, thanks Rose. I probably won't be back until the small hours, and I'll need to sleep. Just leave the key on the hall table when you leave for the train. It was good to see you."

Rose felt the change in atmosphere penetrate her like a chill wind biting into her skin. She hadn't said anything to Kay about the time of the train she was catching the next morning. "Kay, did I say something to upset you?"

Kay didn't answer and left the kitchen. Dismissing the question with a wave from the back of her hand. Rose stared after her. What had just happened?

Rose's phone pinged with a text from Trixie.

Sally's flatmate called. Sally went to London. She didn't say why.

Weird. Was the flatmate worried?

No. She said she hadn't taken her coat

? :-) Did Sally leave the float behind?

No :-(

I misjudged her. She's off to London with my money

Really?

What else? At least she's alright

True

We need someone else and to change the locks on the trailer. Can u put up a social media post pls ?

Sure. NP. Tomorrow :-)

Thanks. CU Tuesday

Rose sent a text to the number she had for Sally. She could wring her neck for just taking off like that without any notice.

Your flatmate told me you were in London. Please contact me about returning the float. Rose.

Rose called the care home before she left. Her father was sleeping, and the care staff reported no change from the day before. As the train made its way through the outskirts of Bristol to London, Rose called the solicitor's office again.

"No-one is in the office today Ms McLaren. Mr Rooney is out of the country on business and Mr Mathers is at Central London Court all day. Yes, we did pass along your message."

Rose sighed as she pressed the button to the call. Why had she promised to follow up with the solicitor when she was in London? There was nothing for it, she would have to try and find Mathers at the court.

Rose took a bus to The Strand and found the posted list of cases being heard that morning in the various court rooms. She knew what Mathers looked like from the website, but there was no listing with his name attached.

All of the listed proceedings were about housing, evictions, and financial claims, which seemed to fit with his speciality. The long corridor with closed wooden doors on either side was imposing. Rose watched the bustling of legal professionals, their clients, couples, and families with small children, as they made their way in and out of the building. The sound of footsteps on the marble floor echoing the sober tones of justice. She had been there for over two hours when she finally spotted Mr Mathers coming out of a courtroom. She recognised him from the photograph on the law firm's website. Balding and bespectacled, he was suited to his profession, a perfect fit for central casting, dark suit and tie, briefcase and sober appearance. The younger fair man he was with looked familiar. She couldn't think where she had seen him before and then she remembered the train station at Perth. Rose drew herself back against the wall and pulled out her camera to take a photograph, following behind the two men as they left the courthouse. The younger man patted Mathers on the back several times, they were both laughing as they climbed into a taxi. The images she captured on her phone were blurred, but she hoped they'd be good enough for face recognition. She enlarged the image. Had she seen him at Perth, the picture wasn't clear enough to be sure. Damn her failing sight. Rose called the solicitor's office. "I've just seen Mr Mathers leaving the courthouse, is he on his way back to the office? This is Rose McLaren again."

"I am not at liberty to give you that information Ms McLaren. Would you like to leave another message for Mr Mathers?"

"Ask him to call me and tell him it's urgent. Say that if he doesn't call me I will have no choice. Thank you."

"No choice?"

"Just tell him that. He'll understand."

Rose clicked off her phone. She was shaking. She had no idea whether the veiled threat, which really didn't mean anything, would make Mathers call her.

Rose sent a text with the image of the two men to Anthony and Mike

Can u identify the young man on the left of this pic? I think I saw him in Perth. The older one is Mathers, the solicitor. I'll explain when I'm back in Edi tomorrow. Tq x

Rose checked her watch. She had agreed to meet Andrea at 3pm. She had enough time to go to Mathers office in case he did go back there, but her instincts guided her against it. There had been no text from Sally. Rose considered what she should do with the spare time. She needed to write down the thoughts that were crowding her head. She wished she hadn't thrown away the map she had started when she first began to explore her concerns about Constance. There was nothing for it, she'd need to buy a new notebook. Paperchase was beckoning.

Rose was on the bus heading to Sloane Square, when Mike's text pinged in.

Can't find him. Nothing online that matches the picture. Sorry.

No worries. Thanks for looking.

Another text, this time from Anthony followed.

Hey, I thought you'd stopped.

I have, I think. It's just that the man with Mathers, I'm sure I saw him recently. I just don't know where. Mike can't find him online.

Did he see you?

No. I've been trying to contact Mathers, but he has ignored my calls so far. He's the solicitor handling the building where Constance lived. The agent you met will know him.

Rose, I've had an odd call from Inspector Hickson. She wants to know where you are. She said she went to the shop on Saturday.

Trixie didn't say. She has my number. Why call you?

I don't know. But you need to be careful. You've said something to make her concerned. Concerned about you I mean.

IDK why! I'll call Hickson. Don't worry.

OK Rose. Today?

Rose frowned. Then pinged back a smiling emoji. What exactly had Hickson told Anthony about their conversation? Her fingers hovered over the keypad, but she didn't press the numbers. Hickson could wait.

Peter Jones Top Floor Brasserie was moderately busy when she arrived. The lunchtime guests had left, and the tea crowd were just beginning to arrive. The smell of food reminded her she hadn't eaten since the night before. She loaded her tray with a vegetarian wrap, coffee, and yoghurt, resisting the baked section, she found a table close to the window, with a spectacular view of Chelsea. Rose hadn't spent very much time in London, and this was only her second time in SW1. The atmosphere felt very different to the West End and where she had been that morning. More Morningside than Haymarket she reflected as she watched a group of age 30 something, glamorous mums in flower print dresses settle their designer clad tiny children into wooden framed highchairs.

Rose began writing in the new notebook she had just bought when Andrea arrived.

"Hello Rose. Sorry, I'm a bit late."

Andrea's lightly made-up face did not hide the dark circles under her eyes. She looked tired and visibly older than when they last met.

"No bother, I was early. Are you alright? Let me get you some tea, or coffee."

Andrea was breathless and put her hand on her chest. "Nothing for me, thanks for coming Rose."

"OK. Why did you want to meet? I told you I wasn't going to ..."

Andrea held up her hand and interrupted Rose. "I know I pressed you to see me. It's about Harry's flat." She blinked back her tears.

"Andrea, what's wrong?"

"Harry's flat, I've had a notice to move. When you rang me and asked about the solicitor, Mathers, I had just received this letter from him, accusing me ..., accusing me of squatting."

Andrea passed a manilla envelope to Rose. It was very like the one sent to Constance's neighbour. Rose pulled out the letter which was attached to another formal document.

"If I don't leave by next weekend they will take me to court."

The words, generous offer, leaped out at Rose as she scanned the letter. "This is their generous offer, to accuse you of squatting and giving you two weeks' notice?"

Andrea's face contorted as she frowned in an effort to hold back the flood of tears that threatened to overwhelm her. "I don't have anything in writing from Harry. My stay at the flat was all agreed on the phone. I knew I would have to move after he died, but this accusation and the threat of court. This is horrible."

"Wait, I thought Mathers was your solicitor?"

"Yes, I met him through Harry. He told me about the debts against the house in Smith Street. He doesn't practice family or divorce law, but he knows about property and financial matters. It was Mathers who advised me to ask for my name to be taken off the title on Smith Street, so no-one could come after me for the loans."

"He told you to give up your house?"

"Well only so that I couldn't be held responsible for William's debts. There was supposed to be a financial settlement, in exchange. But it hasn't materialised yet."

Rose bit her lip. She wasn't a lawyer, and she had no idea of the legal nuances, but something in her gut told her everything about the advice was wrong. She looked at the questions her father's solicitor had told her to ask Mathers and showed them to Andrea.

"Look, it's different, but when I showed some documents about Constance's property in Edinburgh to my father's solicitor, although he thought they looked legit, he suggested I ask some questions. I could phone him, show him a copy of your letter, and see what he suggests if you like. Would it help?"

"Anything Rose. I feel so stupid and helpless."

"Andrea, last time we met, you said you became ill after an accident. What was the accident?"

"Oh, it was stupid, my fault entirely. I used the steps to get a box from the top of a built-in cupboard. The wooden platform broke while I was standing on it. I fell, banged my head, managed to break my hip, and I had a concussion, then the stroke happened. If our cleaner hadn't come on the wrong day, the medics said it would have been touch and go whether I would have made it."

"You and William had separated by then?"

"Well in the middle of it all. I had told him I wanted to sell the house. Which set him off, and he went to stay with a friend overnight. The new girlfriend as I found out later."

"And the cleaner found you?"

"Yes. Normally she didn't come on Thursdays, but she'd taken the Friday off instead. The children were away with the school. I was unconscious by then. She called the ambulance. I was in the hospital for almost nine months. Harry came to see me and told me William had moved the girlfriend into Smith Street. That's when he introduced me to Mr Mathers."

Rose sat back and looked out of the window. Could William have done something to the step ladder?

"Andrea do you have anything from the hospital or the doctors that suggest your fall wasn't an accident?"

"No Rose. It was one of those things. I really should have checked the stepladder before I used it. It was quite old after all."

"All the same, do you mind if I look at the medical notes, if you have them. And the agreement that Mathers created regarding Smith Street."

"Yes, of course. I have the discharge sheet and a letter from the doctor. They're back at the flat. We can go there if you like."

"Sure, but why did you think it wasn't safe for us to meet there?"

"Paranoia. After I received this letter I started to think there were all sorts of conspiracies, that someone was watching me. Fate was coming to get me, like Constance, then Harry and Donna. I know it all sounds so silly."

"I know what it's like to be afraid of shadows, Andrea. How about I get some cake and scones and we take them back to yours? I'd like to get the evening train back to Edinburgh rather than the overnight service."

"Thanks Rose. There's a really good bakery just around the corner, let's get something from there."

Rose watched Andrea as she struggled to balance. She was still shaky on her legs. "How about I go and get the cakes, then come to the flat. You can put the kettle on ready."

"That works. Thanks Rose, you're very thoughtful. I was pretty rotten to you last time."

"I don't remember it like that at all. Now, tell me what sort of a cake you fancy."

Rose studied the cake shop window carefully, they had a grand array of French-style pastries, layered gateaux, cream cakes, macaroons in boxes and specialty biscuits. They must have a very different customer base from my shop in Haymarket, with more money too, Rose reflected, shocked by the prices. She was carrying the beautifully ribboned box carefully up Sloane Street towards Andrea's flat when she felt a pull on her bag. She turned around quickly, ready to kick her assailant. The cake box fell as the first punch landed on the right side of her face. She lost balance and fell, landing awkwardly and, defenceless, she turned to see the sole of a trainer aiming straight at her head. Her normal quick reactions left her as the trainer caught her failing good eye. She tried to curl into a foetal position, but the kicks to her face, body and head kept coming. The edges of her vision blurred and started to go black.

The savage attack was over quickly but Rose was bleeding heavily and losing consciousness.

Someone called an ambulance, but no passer-by had dared to attempt to restrain the attacker as he ran away, fearlessly cutting through traffic, he disappeared down the King's Road.

By the time the ambulance arrived, Rose was already unconscious.

Chapter 10

Trixie was surprised to receive an immediate in person reply to her ad for someone to run the stall. Victoria's enthusiasm for baking and her knowledge had convinced Trixie she was the right person for the job. She was definitely over qualified and more than capable. Both Rob and Trixie really liked her and told her so. She was a Canadian, on an extended holiday. She needed to earn some money to fund her trip to Europe. As a dual national, Victoria also had a British passport, so working wasn't an issue - she could start at the weekend. She had brought references and even offered to stay and help out whilst 'the boss' was away and learn the ropes.

"Aww that's great," Trixie beamed, thrilled to have found someone who appeared to be efficient and almost too perfect, so quickly to replace Sally. "Ah had better run it a' past Rose first. She's a guid woman ye'll like her, but she has the final say. She'll be back on the morrow. Can ye pop back an' meet her then?"

"Sure. Thanks. I'm very excited to possibly be coming to work with you guys. Fingers crossed Rose likes me as much as you two."

"I'm sure she will. It means the stall will be back up and running this weekend. Even though it's short term, until July. Ah know Rose will be relieved, being able to keep it open."

It was just after 4pm when Trixie pinged a text to Rose full of smiling emoji, telling her about Victoria. At the same time Rose was being carefully loaded into the back of an ambulance.

.oOo.

Rose was rushed to the operating theatre as soon as she reached the Chelsea and Westminster A&E. The paramedics knew the head injuries were serious and had potentially nasty consequences.

"Should someone reply to this? Looks like someone who works for her." One of the ambulance crew held up the phone that had fallen out of Rose's bag.

"Better let the police handle it. Poor woman. Why do this, they didn't even take her bag."

But it wasn't the police who told Trixie about Rose's injuries. It was Kay.

"Wha' dae yer mean? I dinnae understand. Why would some monster attack Rose like tha."

"Who knows, it was probably a random attack, a robbery. Although they left her bag. All I know for sure is that Rose is in intensive care, recovering from surgery and she needs rest. They are hoping she will come out of the induced coma tomorrow. Although the blows to her head were really serious, in a way she's been lucky.

"Lucky!" Trixie said it louder than she intended.

"I don't mean lucky it happened, just that, when I spoke to the surgeon he said where she was hit, things could have been way worse."

"OK. Sorry, I didnae mean tae shout Kay."

"You've had a shock Trixie, I get it."

"One o' us should go doon, but I cannae leave the shop."

"It's OK, I've cleared it with the hospital, I'm supposed to be off anyway. I'll go up tomorrow and stay over until Wednesday. I have friends who live nearby and I can stay with them. The police will be in touch with you too. Rose told me she had been looking into someone's death, and then something about a lease. Do you know anything about it? I mean I don't think it could be connected. Do you?"

Trixie took a sharp breath. "She wis looking intae helping a woman aboot her lease. She lived in the same building that a customer who died lived at. The customer used tae own the place. Oh, Ah just wish Rose wouldnae …, it was a couple of years ago when Ah was attacked here in the shop. Rose was involved in trying to find oot aboot a murder. Three murders," Trixie gulped, Kay listened to her sniffling.

"Trixie, I'm so sorry. That sounds horrible. I didn't mean to rake up the past and upset you."

"Ye hav'nae, sorry but it's wha' Ah first wondered when ye told me she had been hurt. Wha' Ah wis always worried aboot, when she'd go poking her nose intae police business. No' that they are all tha' in solving things."

"Look Trixie, you must tell the police everything you know. Just in case there's a connection."

"Ah know. Ah will. Ah'll let Rob an' all the friends know. Will the hospital talk tae me aboot Rose? Ah'm no' her next o' kin."

"Her father can't deal with this, so they will talk to friends as she has no other family. Who else shall I put on the list?"

Trixie gave Kay her full name, Rob's, Marion's and then added Anthony Chatterton. "He was a detective, he's retired an' made friends wi' Rose. Wi' all o' us really."

"Sounds like he might be very helpful. Night Trixie, take care of yourself and call me if you need to."

Trixie put her head between her hands. Could whatever Rose was doing and the attack be connected? Had they tried to kill Rose, the way Troy had? She felt sick and afraid as she locked up the shop. She didn't want to stay there a minute longer. She'd call Rob and Anthony from her boyfriend Graham's flat, she didn't want to be alone, not tonight.

Rob insisted on making the rest of the calls himself. "Trixie, let me call Marion and Anthony. You are too upset, in shock. Take care of yourself. Rose would tell you the same."

Trixie sobbed "Thanks," down the phone and slipped her head onto Graham's shoulder. He pulled her close to him and stroked her hair.

It was almost midnight by the time Rob put the phone down after talking to Anthony, Marion and then to Mike, her partner. He sent Trixie a text.

Everyone knows. Anthony is going to go to London and hope's to talk to the police there. Mike is going to do some digging online about a man Rose had photographed. You OK to open tomorrow? I'll be there early to help.

So Mike and Anthony think there's a connection with what Rose was looking into up here?

No. Not necessarily.

I can't do it Rob. I can't open the shop tomorrow.

I suppose we can close just for a day. But Rose needs us to keep everything going. What about Victoria?

I'll call her. I know. See you Wednesday. xx

Rob stared at the two xx's from Trixie's text. He understood. She was fragile. Rose's assault had brought back horrible memories. But they had to move forward, stay firm. Rose would depend on them more than ever now to keep the business going. And not just the business, if they didn't they would all fall apart. He could feel the fight starting inside. The temptation to numb what he was feeling with alcohol was almost too powerful.

Anthony Chatterton poured himself a large whisky after his call with Rob. He tried to play down the possibility of a connection between the attack and what Rose had been doing, but his instincts told him otherwise. He put a bag together and booked a ticket on the first train out of Waverley to London in the morning. He'd also call Inspector Hickson first thing. From the conversation he'd had with Rose, he doubted Rose would have made calling her a priority and he didn't want whatever Hickson was thinking to grow arms and legs. He wanted to suggest something to Hickson, but it would need a delicate hand. He had been a DCI, he didn't want Hickson thinking he was overly involved and interfering in her work.

Chapter 11

Kay was sitting by Rose's bed when Anthony arrived. Rose was sleeping. Her head and her seeing eye was bandaged, and the lower part of her right arm was covered with a cast.

Kay looked up as he approached the bed. "You must be Anthony, the retired detective. I've heard a lot about you from Trixie and Rose."

"All good I hope. Hello Kay. What an odd and miserable way to meet each other."

Kay nodded. "The police came earlier, but Rose was asleep. They have a few witnesses who saw what happened but apparently whoever who did this was wearing dark clothes. His face was covered with a mask. Honestly, I don't think they have a lot to go on. I thought that area of London would be really safe. And surely there's loads of CCTV."

"Unfortunately, it's not like in films where CCTV handily always catches the person on camera and some obscure admin person recognises them. Police work is a lot harder than film and TV shows make out. I'm sure they'll do their best."

"Of course. It's just that they seemed, well to be honest they weren't very inspiring."

Anthony smiled. "I am fairly sure that's what many people said about me when I turned up to investigate something that had happened. Didn't mean I didn't get to the bottom of things. And sometimes it took a lot longer than I would have liked. Did they look at this?" Anthony pointed to a notebook on the overbed table.

"I don't think so. Why?"

Anthony picked up Rose's notebook and flicked through it. Rose had written a list of names and dates and the beginning of what looked like a family tree. Next to that there was a familiar map in the style of a flight plan, with names instead of countries and various coded links between them. He looked in her bag and found the manilla envelope Andrea had given to Rose. He wondered whether Andrea Summers knew what had happened.

"Kay, do you know if someone called Andrea Summers has called or come to see her? Did the police look at any of this?"

"No. Not while I have been here anyway." Anthony pulled a face. In his opinion it all sounded sloppy, no wonder Kay had described them as uninspiring, but he wasn't about to admit that to Kay.

"I think I'll go and see this Andrea Summers. She must have given these papers to Rose yesterday. I'll come back later. Can I get you some tea or a coffee?" He motioned to a volunteer pouring drinks from an urn just outside the room

"No, I'm fine. So do you think those papers are why Rose was attacked, what about what she was looking into in Edinburgh?"

"Well, possibly it's all connected." He shrugged. "I'm curious why Rose had them, and as the police aren't following it up." He stroked his chin as he tried to remember the conversation he'd had with Rose about Andrea. How did she tie in with Constance and Harry? The beeping from the machine monitoring Rose was strangely reassuring.

Anthony took a taxi over to Sloane Street, but he was out of luck finding Andrea at home. The same doorman who had met Rose when she first called on Andrea was on duty. HIs dual role as a security guard gave him an air of authority rather than deference to most people. Anthony hadn't left the force long enough to lose the aura of policeman and this time he chose not to contradict the assumption. The doorman spoke candidly.

"Did you think it was odd that she didn't leave a forwarding address? What did she say when she left, what do you remember? Please, it's important."

The doorman scratched his head and looked thoughtful. "I was surprised when a taxi van turned up. She had packed three cases and there were two boxes. I asked Mrs Summers where she was going and if I could help. She said no and that she had enjoyed living here. Then she gave me this." He pulled a folded note from his jacket pocket.

Thanks Larry and staff. You've all been very kind. Hope this is enough for a round of drinks. Andrea Summers.

"There was £50 with the note. Very kind of her. She was a nice lady."

Anthony studied the note. It looked as if it had been written in a hurry. He was sure someone like Andrea, living in a fancy place like this, would have proper stationery, not use a scrap torn from a book. He wished he had paid more attention to what Rose had said she was doing in London. She had sent that photograph, who was he? Mike had said he couldn't find any records of the man's face online. Surely no online presence was odd for a man under thirty in this day and age.

"Have you ever seen the younger man, the one on the left in the photo? Do you know if he ever come to see Mrs Summers?" Anthony held up his phone and showed him the picture Rose had taken of the man with the solicitor.

"I have seen the other one before, the older man. He came here to meet Mr Turnbull a few times when he lived here. But not the younger one."

"Thanks, one more thing. A woman who met Mrs Summers yesterday was attacked on the corner of Sloane Street, opposite Peter Jones. It was at about 4 o'clock in the afternoon. What time did Mrs Summers leave here yesterday; when she took her bags I mean."

"Oh, that's easy, just before seven. I was going off shift and William the night man was taking over. I heard about the attack on the news. Not something that happens around here. Shocking. I didn't know the lady was a friend of Mrs Summers."

"Mrs Summers didn't have any visitors yesterday then?"

"No. She did go out, in the middle of the afternoon."

"Do you remember the name of the taxi, you said it was a taxi van?"

"Sorry, I don't. Be a local firm though. There's a firm on Ebury Street some of the residents use if they need something bigger than a black cab, or a driver for the day. They have posh cars too. And usually, we'd be the ones to book a car, but yesterday Mrs Summers did it herself."

"Thanks. This is my number if you can think of anything else, or if Mrs Summers happens to get in touch for any reason."

"I thought you were the police." The doorman looked disappointed when Anthony didn't produce a professional card.

"I was, but I recently retired."

"Well, you fooled me, but then I never asked you did I." The man smiled at his own folly. "Look I shouldn't have …"

Anthony held up his hand. "I know and I won't be telling anybody that you spoke to me. Don't worry."

Anthony stopped in at a sandwich shop then made his way back over to the hospital. "Here, I didn't know if you had had a chance to eat," he said, handing one of the sandwich bags to Kay.

"Thanks, but I'm vegetarian and I…"

"I guessed. It's avocado and roast veggies. Hope that's ok."

"Oh my, you are a good detective to have known that."

Anthony smiled. "Alright, I confess. Rose told me, we talked when she was staying with you. Has she woken up at all?"

They both turned to look at Rose. She looked comfortable enough but there was no sign of activity. The steady beeping filled the room as they observed their friend. A nurse bustled in to check her vitals.

"Not yet, the doctor came in and he seems happy enough to leave her for now. There's no brain swelling which is good, but she took a kick to the eye. Another consultant, an eye specialist, is supposed to be coming to see her."

Anthony closed his eyes, remembering the conversation in Rose's hallway after her birthday dinner. She hadn't told him what else was bothering her, but he had had a strong feeling it was something to do with her sight. "Let's hope he comes soon. Look, you've been here most of the day. I'm happy to stay on."

"I was hoping you would be able to figure out why this happened."

"I am going to try, but as I said before, police work, especially for an old retired and methodical policeman like me, takes time."

Once Kay left, Anthony studied the list of names Rose had written and tried to make sense of the codes she had used in her map. He sent a text to Mike.

Can you forward me the messages you and Rose exchanged. It might help me pull some pieces together. I'm with her now. She's still sleeping.

Sure. I'll forward them now.

Antony looked at his watch. He still preferred the old fashioned timepiece to checking his phone. It was already seven, the hospital was still busy, with visitors and staff weaving in an endless stream in and out of the rooms. The sun was beginning to set, casting an orange glow across the paper he was writing on, next to the bed where Rose lay.

Constance Brown = Dead
Harry Turnbull = Dead
Donna Meikle = Dead
William Summers/Andrea Summers?
Mathers and Rooney?
Property/Investments?
Man in Picture with Mathers?
Perth?
Canadian cousin?

Hoping for a pattern to emerge Anthony stared at the words on the page. What had Rose seen, why had she circled Perth and connected it to the Canadian cousin and Harry Turnbull? He was about to try and find the taxi firm that had picked up Andrea Summers when Trixie called.

"How is she?"

"Still asleep Trixie. She's in good hands. How are you coping?"

"OK. We didnae open today, but Rob an' Ah'll be back at the shop tomorrow. Dae ye think … Dae ye think Rose is gonnae die Anthony?" She let out a huge sob.

"No Trixie, no. Take a breath. Rose is not as bad as everyone first thought. The operation went really well. She's going to be fine." Now wasn't the time to tell Trixie how worried he was about Rose's injury to her good eye. "Rose would want everything to continue on, especially the shop. It's her livelihood, yours too and Rob's."

"Ah noo, Ah just feel sae terrible for her, an' …"

"And what Trixie?"

"Wha happened before. I cannae stop thinking aboot it."

"Trixie listen to me. That was terrible, and Rose would never ask you to do anything that put you in harm's way again. You do know that don't you?"

"Ay, o' course. Ye're right Ah'm sorry. I found someone tae help, tae replace Sally. Do ye think Ah should just make the decision to hae her help oot.?"

"What happened to Sally? She ran the stall right?"

"Ay, and then last weekend, she locked it up and went away tae London o' all places. Took the float wi' her."

"Last weekend? While Rose was away?"

"Ay."

Anthony paused.

"Ye still there?"

"Yes, sorry I was just curious, wondering why she had done that. She seemed to really fit in and I thought she was at university?"

"Ay, that's wha's so odd."

"Trixie, I don't want to speak for Rose. She trusts you and you need to trust yourself to make the right decision."

"Okay. Ah will. Can ye tell Rose we're wantin' her back as soon as she's able an' not tae worry in the meantime."

"I will Trixie. And I'll let you know what's happening. Take care now."

Anthony scratched his head and looked back at the list. It had to be a coincidence that Sally had gone awol, but he didn't like coincidences and his gut told him something different. "Oh Rose, I wish you'd wake up. I need you to help me, help you, to figure out whatever this mess of a puzzle is."

"Anthony?" A faint voice murmured from the bed.

"Rose, yes, it's me. You're awake! I'll call the nurse."

For the next half an hour Anthony waited in the corridor as the medical staff did their checks. The eye consultant appeared in the middle of it all. A tall and gangly figure with white hair and very long fingers. The two doctors spent a long time discussing their patient with each other. There were various nods of agreement across Rose's bed and their body language signalled problems. Anthony wished Kay was here, as a doctor they might talk to her more openly than they would to him.

Finally, they came out and spoke to him. "Are you a relative?"

"No, her only living relative, her father is in a care home, he has dementia. I'm a retired policeman, a friend. Is she going to be alright?"

"Yes, much better than we first thought, except …"

"Her eye?"

The eye specialist shifted. "It's too soon to say, but we may need to do another operation, to try and save what sight she had left. I'll come and check again tomorrow, there's too much swelling at the moment for me to test her properly."

Anthony froze. "Could she be …, I mean, this has made things worse."

"Definitely. How much do you know about her sight loss?"

"That she is already blind in one eye and that the other eye is beginning to fail too."

"This injury may mean a complete change of how she lives her life. She is young and she will be able to take advantage of all sorts of support, but it won't be easy."

"If anyone can overcome difficulty, Rose can. She's been through ...,"

"Yes, I saw that from her records. I'll be back to take another look tomorrow. I'll know more then."

Anthony went back to sit with Rose. "How are you Rose?"

Rose sighed deeply. "I'm falling apart Anthony and I brought it on myself."

"What do you mean?"

"You all warned me, Trixie, Rob, you. You all told me not to look for trouble. If only I had listened, maybe I wouldn't be lying here now."

Anthony was shocked, this was unlike Rose. The depth of feeling in her words, made her sound so lost, so different from the resilient and strident woman he had come to know. He wanted to tell her everything would be alright, but he didn't want to lie. And he knew she would be able to tell if he did. Sight or no sight, Rose could always tell a faker. "What can I do Rose?"

"I don't know. I want to say get the bugger who did this to me, but I ..."

"Rose, you didn't bring this on yourself. No-one deserves to be hurt like you have been. But I have to ask you, do you think this is to do with why you were in London, or something else?"

"Definitely connected to what's going on now. Oh my, did you think ...? Rose's thoughts turned to the murders at the Edinburgh Fringe and the man behind everything that had happened last summer. The man who had gotten away with murder.

He read her thoughts, "It crossed my mind."

Rose moved her head slowly from side to side. "I can't nod properly, but no, I'm pretty sure the reason I am here is to do with Constance, Harry and Donna. Their deaths are somehow connected to that building in Edinburgh and the flat that Andrea Summers was living in. It belonged to Harry. I have the papers and a letter Andrea gave me."

"I know, I read them. I went to see Andrea, but she's gone."

"What do you mean?"

"Last night, after you were attacked she left, in a hurry. From the note she gave to the doorman, she isn't going back there. If you have the energy, you'd better tell me everything you know, or think you know, Rose."

It was after 8pm when Anthony finally left Rose's side. She had talked him through her map, why she was convinced Constance's death was not an accident and the conversations she had had with Andrea, with William Summers and Donna Meikle.

"And that detective, Hickson, how well do you know her?"

"Not well. It seems like you two didn't hit it off."

"No, we didn't. Honestly, I have a feeling she thinks I had something to do with Donna's death."

Anthony didn't say anything. He had had the same feeling. "So best I get to work and clear the good name of Rose McLaren then."

"Oh I'm glad you think it's funny. But yes, I think you better have. You'll need my phone to transfer some of the pictures. I don't fancy any more time in police custody or worse. Thank you for coming and... Please, be careful."

"Goodnight Rose. I'll see you tomorrow."

Chapter 12

Anthony called Rob and then Trixie to update them. He was on his way back to the B & B on Fulham Road. The digs were close to the hospital, cheap for London and clean, but that was about all that could positively be said for the place. The outside of the building needed serious repair work and the plumbing in the shared bathroom burbled and hissed like a geezer.

He hadn't been in London for years. All his old contacts and friends had either retired or transferred to forces outside of London. Apart from his ex wife. He wandered further down Fulham Road, towards The Star. The old pub was no longer a local or a coppers boozer. It had been retrofitted, competing for young and fashionable gastro pub customers. He downed two pints and picked at the salad he had asked for, instead of chips, to go with the burger. Trying to lose more weight, after his last consultation with a doctor, was a challenge. He felt lacklustre. Despite his promise to Rose, he still wasn't convinced by her theory about what had happened to Constance Brown. Hickson had agreed to his suggestion. It went in her favour to get the tests done if she was serious about Rose being involved. What on earth had Rose said to make Hickson think Rose had something to do with Donna Meikle's crash?

.oOo.

Rose had a difficult time settling after Anthony left. Despite the cautious answers the eye doctor had confirmed her worst fears. She had lived with the possibility that she would be legally blind by the time she was in her mid forties, but that day had come already. Her head was spinning. She felt angry. No money in the world could buy back what she had lost, never mind what she was about to lose. She wished she hadn't told Anthony to take her phone. She needed to call Rob, he would understand how close she was to giving up. Everytime she closed her eyes her mind was haunted by the dreams she had been having, the dead horses, Troy with the gun. It was after 4am by the time she finally fell asleep.

"How are you this morning Rose? I was so happy when they told me you had woken up, after I left yesterday ."

The nursing staff had disturbed her earlier to do their observations, and she had fallen back asleep. She gave Kay a faint smile and lifted the arm without the cast up. Her thumb was turned down. She shrugged. "I'm not gonnae lie to you Kay. I feel like crap inside and out. Did you speak to Anthony last night? Is that why you're here?"

"No. I came yesterday morning. You were sleeping. Should I have spoken to him?"

"I just wondered if he'd filled you in about the good doctors."

"No. He didn't call me. What did they say? You're doing well Rose. I mean, those head injuries, it's a miracle that you're as …"

"It's my eye." Rose interrupted. "I'm probably not going to be able to see ever again."

Kay put her hand to her mouth and looked down. "Oh Rose. Are you sure that's what they said? Surely it's too early for them to be definite about that?"

"I know what they meant."

"Do you want me to speak to them, find out what I can?"

"I'm not a child. I can ask, speak for myself."

"I know, it's …, I'm sorry Rose. I didn't mean to insult you."

"Yeah, well people do that don't they. They take over your life, thinking they know best. And when you have something good to tell them, if it doesn't suit them for some reason they get moody and ignore you."

"Rose what are you talking about?"

"You know what."

"Is this about how I behaved when you told me about the money your Dad left you?"

Rose nodded.

"I'm sorry. I know, I was an idiot. I don't know what came over me. I think I was, to be really honest, jealous. I had planned to call you to apologise when all this happened and I found out you had been attacked."

"How did you find out?"

"The police contacted the care home, they traced your Dad and the care home told them to call me because they knew you had stayed with me. I explained to the police your only living relative was your Dad. They seemed OK to speak to me, giving me the details about where you were …, sometimes having the doctor title means I get to know things and go places. Rose, please believe me, I am really sorry about the way I acted when you told me about the money, what your Dad had done for you."

Rose stretched her hand over the covers of the bed, palm upwards. Kay brought her hand down to meet it and gave Rose's hand a gentle squeeze.

Rose considered what Kay had said. She wasn't sure she quite believed the story, but whatever else the reason might have been Kay had more than made up for her behaviour by coming to the hospital. "Jealousy is a monster isn't it? I've been guilty of it too. Sometimes it takes me over and I can't think straight or rationally. Then I don't appreciate what I have at all - I just focus on what other people have."

"Yes. That's what happened, on Sunday. I only saw what I didn't have. Being cut off by my family."

Rose was about to reply when the eye doctor breezed in. "Good Morning ladies. Now Rose, I am going to take a peek under the dressing and see about that swelling. It's all looking a lot better than yesterday from the outside. OK?" His upbeat and cheerful manner broke the tension.

"This is my friend Kay, she's also a doctor. Mind if she stays, while you tell me the worst?"

"From the looks of your face, I'm hoping I have something positive to say. Yes, if you want to stay." He nodded towards Kay, then leaned in to look more closely at his patient. Rose breathed in, holding the tension in her body as she felt him removing the dressing and exhaling slowly. He held up two fingers in front of her eye.

"What do you see?"

"Two fingers. Oh my God, Oh my God!" Her body shuddered as relief overwhelmed her. "I can still see."

The doctor placed a hand on her shoulder and peered closely at the wounds to her face. "Someone was watching over you Rose, a millimetre to the left and things would have looked very different. We couldn't tell before, with all the swelling. I'd like to do some tests tomorrow and follow up with your doctor in Edinburgh. The way things are going, my guess is you'll be out of here in a couple of days."

"I could kiss you right now. Everyone, I could kiss everyone. An hour ago, I couldn't see the point going on, now I want to …"

"Fly to the moon?" said Kay, squeezing Rose's hand.

"Almost, but no. I feel like what happened has shown me something I needed to learn."

"Really?"

"I was holding on so tightly to the past. I think that was why I was having such horrible dreams."

"I still hope they find and prosecute whoever did this to you."

"Yeah, me too. I'm not that nice." Rose's laugh came from deep inside her belly.

"Well before you get two carried away, there's some things I need you to do, to keep the wound clean." The doctor handed her a Perspex eye shield and some drops. "Wear this and put these in, four times a day. You know how?"

Rose nodded. "Yes, thank you."

"I'll see you tomorrow. Keep laughing. It's good for you." He said as he swept out of the room.

"He's quite the personality."

"I like him more than my dour guy in Edinburgh. Kay, do you have a mirror? I'd like to see how bad I look."

"Are you sure that's a good idea? It's mostly bruising, and your head is still bandaged."

"I need to see."

"OK, here, I have a mirror on my phone."

Rose was studying herself when Anthony arrived carrying cups of coffee, fruit and pain au chocolat.

"You can see?"

"Yep," she grinned.

"What did the doctor say?"

Rose filled him in with the details and the good news she would be able to leave the hospital. "These are sooo good," she said as she took a mouthful of the flaky pastry. "Maybe we should start making them at Morrison Street, although I've always been better at baking cakes than pastry."

"Cold hands," said Kay. "That's what my dadi, my Dad's mum, always said anyway."

"Glad you like them. Rose, is there anywhere you could go for a while, instead of coming back to Edinburgh I mean?"

"Why would I go anywhere else Anthony? I want to go home."

"Look, this mugger, it wasn't random Rose I'm sure of it. I'm worried. Whoever did this, might know where you live."

"I'll get an alarm fitted. No-one is going to keep me away from where I want to be. Have the right to be."

Anthony held up his hands. "I agree with you, but just until they catch him."

"But without me, they might not catch him and Anthony, I want him caught. Whoever did this you're right, it was intended. I intend to not let them get away with it. I'm certainly not going to hide."

Anthony sighed and pulled out Rose's notebook from a bag, along with some loose paper which he'd made his own notes on.

"The puzzle?" Kay asked.

"Yeah. Rose, I think I owe you an apology."

"It's fine, you just wanted to make sure I was safe."

"I didn't mean that. I mean about Constance, Harry and Donna."

"Tell me what you think."

Anthony spread the papers onto the overbed table and opened up Rose's notebook to the map she had started. "They didn't do a tox screen on Constance because they assumed her death was from a fall, or on Harry because he hanged himself and there was a suicide note. They did do one for Donna because they first assumed she was drunk, then because she had taken something. Something, by the way, that you gave her."

"What?"

"It's ok, Hickson now realises you didn't."

"For goodness sakes, how on earth could she have thought … Sorry. Carry on."

"I had suggested to Hickson that she request tests on Constance and Harry as a way of proving you couldn't have had anything to do with what happened to Donna. It was something I would have done. Look what came back." He showed her the text from Inspector Hickson.

Can't reveal what, but you were right. Same substance found in all three. I hope Rose makes a good recovery.

Rose put her hand to her mouth. "Drugs of some sort. Poison?"

"She can't say, but the tox reports, same substance whatever it is, that's not a coincidence. Whoever is behind the deaths thinks they have got away with it."

"Murder by stealth," muttered Rose. "So now we need to figure out why?"

"My guess is financial. We should look at who gains. Does this mean you want to carry on, find out what happened?"

"Oh yeah! Donna's brother William is the most likely suspect, he's broke, but I don't see him murdering his sister, and apart from her house, after the business lost it's capital, she didn't have a fortune to leave him. Neither Harry or Constance had any children or direct heirs and their wills named each other as the beneficiary. But again, after the company dissolved, where did the money go? What they did have left goes to horse charities and good causes. There was a small beneficiary from Constance to the Canadian cousin, but not enough to commit murder for. Harry left Andrea Summers £5,000. And Andrea had that accident, which ..." Rose faltered as she caught the look on Anthony's face.

"How on earth did you get access to the wills?"
Rose bit her lip. "Probably best if I don't say."
"Marion?"

Rose looked down. "Let's just say I know someone who …"

"Mike."

Rose flushed. "I knew you wouldn't approve."

"You'd be right."

The was an awkward silence.

Kay coughed, she had sat watching the conversation, and interjected, "Look, you two have a lot to talk about and I'm not good at this sort of thing at all. I'm going to leave and head back to Bristol, now that I know you're OK Rose. If you do decide not to go back to Edinburgh, you're more than welcome to stay with me. And, of course, anytime you come down to see your Dad."

"Thanks Kay. I'm glad we got things sorted out earlier."

"Me too Rose. Take care."

Anthony looked stern, "Ground rules Rose, remember, nothing illegal if you want me to help you."

"I do, but outside of the police Anthony, the only way to find things out is bending the rules."

"Hacking isn't just bending the rules, Rose."

"I know. But, did you never bend them, all the time you worked for the police I mean. You never did one thing, even slightly outwith procedure, to get a result?"

Anthony sighed. "Ok Rose, fair do's. But I …"

"Agreed. Now, let's see if we can make sense of what we know. I need to call Andrea Summers too. I don't suppose she knows why I didn't turn up with the cakes."

"She does, I was going to tell you. Well, I assume she does because three hours after you were attacked she left the flat and isn't coming back."

"What do you mean?"

"I went over to the flat, you were sleeping. I looked at the papers in your bag and realised from your notes that you and she had met the same day. You just mentioned an accident?"

"She told me about a fall, before she left her husband, she claims it was an accident, a broken stepladder, and then she had a stroke. She said we shouldn't meet at the flat because she was afraid, but then we were going back there anyway to look at her medical report and a couple of other papers."

"So you were on your way to meet her when you were attacked."

"Yes, we had been to Peter Jones just before that, then I went to the cake shop."

"Did you see anyone in Peter Jones, sense anyone following you?"

"No. Andrea said she thought someone was keeping an eye on her, but then she dismissed it as silly. To be honest I thought it was anxiety because of the eviction letter. She said she thought she might be the next victim. Oh why didn't I take it more seriously. I should have asked her who."

"Do you know where she might go? The doorman had no idea and when I called the taxi company they told me they had taken her to Paddington Station. Although it sounded as if she had quite a bit of luggage."

"Left luggage? Maybe she stored it there? I'm a bit tired ... Do you fancy making a trip to see?"

Anthony smiled. "OK boss. Do you need anything before I go?"

"No, it's fine. The food here isn't bad, but a pain au chocolat, if you find one, would be great with a cup of tea later. I'm going to figure out a recipe and ask Trixie to trial it. I'm thinking hazelnuts or walnuts, blended with really good dark chocolate and a hint of cream."

Chapter 13

Rose sent Trixie a brief text with the latest news about her recovery and when she would likely be back at work, then decided to call her. It was easier than texting and it would be good to hear Trixie's voice.

"Aww Rose, it's sae good to hear ye."

"You too Trixie, that's why I called. But, I may not make much sense."

"Nae bother. I wanted tae know if I can tell the lass, the one who came in yesterday for the job, if she can start? Her references are excellent an' Ah think she'll be really guid. She'll be here, in Edinburgh, until July. Rob likes her tae."

"Yes, of course. I trust you Trixie. Well done finding someone so quickly. You're a star. Do what you need to do to keep going. But don't take on too much. We can reduce opening if we have to."

"Nae, no need."

"Well, forget the trailer if need be, and have her work in the shop, if it's too much. Rob can help serve and we can organise transport for the deliveries. I'll send you a template for a temporary contract for her. Same wages as Sally. We need to talk about a raise for you as well."

"Dinnae fash. Just get better. An' soon."

"I will. Thanks so much for keeping things going and everything."

Rose leaned her head back against the pillow. She was exhausted but the fog in her head was beginning to clear. She was beginning to be able to process information again. Making literal sense out of the multiple facets, like a diamond cutter faced with a unique stone. The first cut could make the difference between priceless and worthless.

.oOo.

Anthony took the bus from Kings Road to Fulham Broadway and the District line over to Paddington. He knew the route well. He had once been stationed at Paddington Green. The station was bustling. He looked at the departure board. Andrea could be anywhere by now, have left the country even. Paddington had a high speed link to London Heathrow. But, if she was hiding her tracks, Rose's hunch she might have left her bags here didn't mean she travelled from here. She could have gone to a different station, there were so many choices. He knew, without access to CCTV, he'd need to go back to old fashioned detective methods to figure it out.

The left luggage was run by an independent company a few hundred yards from the station. They also sold food, luggage and a variety of items to attract the eye of their travelling customers. A young couple were checking in their bags when Anthony arrived. The clerk behind the desk was also young, Australian from the sound of his accent. By the way Rose had described Andrea, it didn't seem likely that she could manage more than one suitcase and a handbag given she used a stick. The doorman had indicated she'd had a lot more luggage than that. He looked around the shop. He thought his best chance was to try and talk to the clerk casually rather than direct questions. He picked up a pair of women's socks and waited for the young couple to finish their deposit.

"Can I help?" The clerk reached out his hand for the socks.

"Uh, I think so. Not sure if you were on last night, around 7 or 8pm?"

"Yeah. It sucked. My mate called in sick, so I had to double shift."

"That's too bad. You from Aus?"

"Yeah, working holiday. I'm off to Ibiza next week. Sun, girls and well you know what they say."

Anthony chuckled. "Ah, that sort of holiday was a long time ago for me."

The clerk grinned. "Did you want those socks mate, not sure they're your size."

"Well actually they're for my wife. She managed to drop her spare pair when she checked in her luggage last night. I was hoping you might have found them. They were pale pink, like these, but without the flamingos."

"Right. Nah, I didn't see any socks. What's she look like, your wife?"

Anthony described Andrea.

"Yeah, I remember her. The taxi driver loaded everything in before I could stop him. We don't take that sort of load. Didn't she tell you?"

"Oh, she probably has, but I didn't listen. Typical. She's always telling me off about that. So you didn't store anything here?"

"No. It all went back outside. It was busy so I didn't see what happened after that. You'd better call her."

"Well, I would, that's the other problem, I have lost my phone. And she's on her way to visit our friends. I'm getting a later train. Any other storage place round here that would take the bags?"

"Yeah, about fifteen minutes walk. It's a locker service. They have bigger lockers than we do. We're really for backpackers or people in London for a day or two with a big suitcase they don't want to lug around with them. Your wife had boxes and all sorts."

"Yes, we're in the middle of moving and she wanted to take some things to our friends. I think she packed way too much. Thanks anyway, I'll try the other place."

"You taking the socks?"

"Yes, why not, they're quite fun aren't they." Anthony hoped Rose would like them as he tucked the small parcel into his coat pocket and headed over to the other storage facility. It was odd that the taxi company hadn't mentioned a second trip. But then he hadn't thought to ask. He chuckled, his story had been anything but consistent, but the clerk hadn't seemed to notice and to his surprise, he'd quite enjoyed making things up on the spot.

He was just turning onto North Wharf Street when he saw a woman who fitted Andrea's description hailing a black cab, outside a hotel. She had a large suitcase and was leaning on a stick. Anthony ran towards her.

"Wait, please. Andrea, I can help you. I'm a friend of Rose."

Her face contorted as she looked up. "Go away, leave me alone."

The driver of the cab had pulled over and was getting out to help with the bag. "You heard the lady. Now bugger off."

Anthony put his hands up. "OK, look Andrea, someone attacked Rose, I can see that you're frightened. But where will running get you? You'll always be looking over your shoulder."

"You're Rose's policeman friend aren't you?"

"Yes. Retired."

Andrea sighed. "Sorry driver. I've changed my mind."

"OK lady, if you're sure." The cabbie gave Anthony a look that could kill.

Anthony lifted the case out of the cab and helped Andrea back inside the hotel. There was a small cafe to the left of the reception. "Shall we sit there and talk?"

"Sure, but I don't know what to tell you."

Anthony put the tray with two coffees and an assortment of sandwiches, crisps and fruit on the table. "I wasn't sure what you liked, and you looked like you could do with some food."

"I'm not sure when I last ate. Rose was going to bring some cakes to my flat when she was attacked."

"So you do know what happened. Do you know who, and why?"

Andrea shook her head. She was trembling and pulled her jacket tight. "You have to believe me, I don't know, but whoever it was, I need to get away. I think they're after me too. The same person who killed all the others is coming for me."

Anthony stretched his arm across the table. "Why would someone want to kill you Andrea, or Constance and Harry and Donna. You must have some idea. Even if it's a thought you think is too ridiculous to say out loud."

"I really don't. When I met Rose she asked me about the accident, when I fell off the step ladder at my house in Smith Street. I think she thought that wasn't an accident. But the only person who could have tampered with the ladder is William, my ex husband. He's a philanderer and an idiot with money, but he's not a murderer."

"Murder can be committed by anyone, I've met some surprisingly respectable ones. But these murders have to have been planned very carefully. Does that sound like something William is capable of?"

"Not at all. William couldn't plan what underwear to put on, if it wasn't put out for him. I did that for years. Now he has someone new to take care of life's minutiae."

"When did you last see him, or speak to him?"

"I don't remember, I think it was after I saw Rose. I called him because I needed to know what was happening about the settlement. That's when he told me the money from the company that Harry and Constance owned had gone. That it was missing."

"Missing? So he does have a motive. How much was he expecting?"

"He was giving me £250,000, that's all I know. And the money was there. Mathers had assured me of that when he told me to sign the document, giving William the Smith Street house."

Anthony frowned. "Mathers, but I thought he was trying to evict you?"

"Yes, he is now, but before, he was my solicitor. I didn't realise he didn't still represent me. Seems like he took me for a fool."

"Have you ever seen this man before?" He held up the picture Rose had taken outside the courthouse.

Andrea put her head to one side and stared at the image. "Well isn't that the darndest thing. He looks like Harry, when he was young I mean."

"Harry Turnbull?"

"Yes, from that profile, that's who he reminds me of. But I have no idea who he is."

Anthony pulled out his phone and studied the image of the notes he had taken at the B&B. Donna had told Rose that there had been a rumour that Harry and Constance had had a child together. Donna had been bothered by a photograph, which is when she left the cafe. "Did you ever hear a rumour about Harry and Constance having a child together?"

"No. I don't remember anyone saying that. Harry was a catch, but he never married. That said, it wouldn't surprise me if there were some little Harry's running about."

Anthony looked at the photograph again, then a photograph of Harry that Rose had sent him. He didn't see the resemblance, but then the picture of Harry was of a much older man.

"I need to go Anthony, I really don't feel safe in London. I stored some things at a deposit near here. But I didn't have any specific plan."

"Where were you going in the taxi?"

"Sounds stupid now, but I was going to Victoria Station and take the Gatwick Express. Then I was going to book an affordable flight to somewhere in Europe. Somewhere where I could think, sit in the sun to heal. The last few months have been awful."

"Rose told me you had had a stroke after the fall. Would you take a risk, trust me to look out for you for a couple more days? I think Rose would like to talk with you. I'm in a pretty awful B&B on Fulham Road. It's cheap and it's clean. Then you could take off to your sunspot. Rose will be leaving the hospital and I'll take her back to Edinburgh."

"I do trust you and Rose especially, but I'd rather be on my way. I can talk to Rose by phone. I bought a new one, in case anyone was tracking my old number. I think they can do that nowadays. Here, I'll message you with it."

Anthony told her his number and she connected. "This number will be between you, me and Rose. I promise."

"Thanks Anthony. I'll call you before I leave Gatwick."

He helped her with the case and hailed a taxi, which they shared to Victoria station. He wanted to make sure she made the next train safely. Then he headed back to the hospital. He knew Rose was not going to be happy Andrea had left, but he had no way of forcing the woman to stay. And he got it. She was terrified.

Rose had been moved out of intensive care to a private room on a general ward when Anthony arrived. She was growing impatient and wanted to leave. "They want to keep me one more night, but I don't see the point. I mean, I've just done more tests and everything is looking good. I'm sure someone else could use this bed."

Anthony smiled, did women not need looking after and protecting nowadays? His father would be turning in his grave. He had been old fashioned, chivalrous and tried to wrap his wife in cotton wool, which she had joked about, until her death ten years ago. Their marriage had been happy and his mum had cried tears of joy when he tied the knot and married Jan. He was glad his mother hadn't known he and Jan split up. His father died five years later, he seemed to just give up after he lost his wife. Anthony thought he died from a broken heart. He wrestled with his thoughts, wanting to protect Rose and knowing she would hate that. He had grown fond of the woman, like the daughter he never had.

"Rose, if they're suggesting you stay, there must be a reason. What harm could another day of recovery and rest do?"

"I can't just abandon Trixie and Rob to manage everything. I need to be there. I can at least do all the admin support and ordering from home until I feel able to take on the cooking and I'd like to meet this new staff member, Victoria, before she gets too settled. Anthony, we've also got work to do. I don't think we can solve anything from down here, although I would have liked to meet that solicitor Mathers. How did you get on with finding Andrea?"

"She's on her way to somewhere hot."

"What?"

"I'll fill you in, I have a new phone number for her. She's terrified, Rose. That's why she left the flat in such a hurry. Look, why don't we stay one more day, and I'll try and see if I can meet Mathers. I can approach him about the

Edinburgh flats, nothing to do with Andrea Summers or you."

"Are you suggesting subterfuge Anthony? Making up stories?" Rose laughed.

"Mmm, I'm beginning to rather enjoy it."

He checked his watch. It was already after 3pm. "If I leave now, I could get over to his office by 4pm."

"Go on then, I hope he's there."

"By the way, the photograph you took of the man with Mathers, Andrea said he reminded her of a younger Harry. Maybe you could get Mike to look into that while I'm gone."

"Oh keep the big news to last, why don't you!" She screwed up a piece of paper and threw it at him, smiling. "Now go, find that sneaky solicitor. Thanks partner."

Rose took a breath. Had Anthony just changed her mind for her? The old fears about trust and relying on someone shook her. "Stop it," she said aloud. "You don't help me." One of the housekeeping staff appeared with a cup of tea and biscuits and gave her a menu to choose from for supper. Rose remembered the pain au chocolat she had asked Anthony to bring her earlier. Instead, he had found Andrea and a glimmer of a clue that might help.

Hiya Mike. Anthony just said the younger man in the photo I sent looks like Harry Turnbull when he was younger. I don't have any of the news clippings here. Could u c what u can find. Does Harry have a son? Why isn't he in the will?

On it. R u getting better?

TQ yes much. Home tomorrow!

She opened the notebook to the map she had started, drew in another circle with a question mark and connected it to Harry.

An hour after he had left Rose at the hospital Anthony found himself walking up and down a historic alley three times before he finally found the discreet sign for the offices of 'Rooney and Mathers'. Spitalfields had been developed and modernised since his last visit, as a policeman. He was unfamiliar with the new street layout. The glass tower blocks dwarfed the old buildings and many of the familiar landmarks were gone. The old alley was now full of restaurants, specialty shops selling expensive chocolates, art and handmade jewellery. The wine bar, underneath the solicitors offices, was packed with suited men and fashionable young women.

"Can I help you?" A tall brunette was standing behind the reception desk as he pushed open the door of the solicitors offices on the third floor. There was no lift and Anthony was slightly breathless as he arrived.

"I hope so, I'm looking for Mr Mathers, is he available?"

"I am afraid not. Mr Mathers is only available by appointment. And he is currently already engaged."

"I see, well can I make an appointment? When might he next be free?"

"Mr Mathers appointment diary is full. He isn't taking on any new clients."

"How do you know I am a new client?"

The woman pursed her lips. "I haven't seen you before. I make all Mr Mathers appointments."

"It was a friend who recommended Mr Mathers. Are you sure he won't be annoyed if you turn me down, without checking with him?"

"I have very clear instructions from Mr Mathers. However, if you leave your name and a phone number, I will check with him Mr ..., who was it who referred you?"

"Mr Turnbull, Harry Turnbull."

The woman was well trained. Her poker face remained flat. "And you are?"

Anthony hesitated, "Chatterton. Anthony Chatterton. Do you have a pen? I can write down my number and leave a message for Mr Mathers."

"He isn't coming back today, so you'll have to tell me the message."

Whoever she was, she was good at protecting her employer, Anthony thought. What did he pay for such loyalty and why? "OK, just my number then. Please let him know it is important."

Chapter 14

"Hey Rob," Trixie looked up from the text on her phone and opened the back door of the shop. "Rose will be back the morra."

"Brilliant," he paused, unloading the afternoon deliveries from the bike." Do we know how she really is?"

"Nae, ye know Rose. An' she's already creating new recipes. She's gone all fancy doon south an' wants tae include pain au chocolat."

"Ooh I love those. Her version will be even better I'm sure."

Trixie gave him an eye roll before going back into the kitchen, muttering, "But she's nae the one daein' the cookin'. Thank the lord fer you Victoria, the biscuits look guid."

"Thanks Trixie, the recipe is easy enough. I hope you don't mind, I added some lemon to the icing on the thumbprints. It helps enhance the raspberry."

Trixie pursed her lips. "Ah dinnae think we should change things while Rose is away. Have ye iced them?"

"Yes. I'm sorry."

"Dinnae fash, just ask me next time. Rob can tak ye over tae the stall and Ah'll get prepped for tomorrow. Ye guid wi' that?"

"Sure, and I'm really sorry about the lemon."

Rob came through the kitchen and helped himself to one of the biscuits Trixie had put out for tasting. "Any news from Sally?"

"Rose hasnae heard from her."

"I can't believe it. It seems so unlike her to just take off like that."

"Her mum left a message earlier, she's nae heard from her and Ah think she's starting to get worried. She said something aboot the police. Ah let Rose know."

"You know, I took off for three months once. My mom was furious. I met a boy, fell in love and headed over to the USA on a ferry with him. It just happened. It took me at least two weeks to call my mom – and that was only because his mom realised I hadn't told anyone where I was. She saw a news report that I was missing. I'm sure Sally will turn up and be fine."

"Ah hope so Victoria. Now yer twa better heed off, oot of ma road, and look at the stall."

"Yes Trixie, anything you say Trixie, three bags full. You're certainly getting used to being in charge Trixie," Rob laughed as he and Victoria headed out the door.

Despite Victoria's well meaning reassurances about Sally, Trixie was worried. She knew only too well what could happen if Sally had taken something she didn't know how to handle. Sally had always said she didn't experiment with drugs, but there was always a first time. And if someone had slipped something into her drink ...

Thinking like that wasn't going to help. She'd ask Graham to go with her that night and see if they could find anyone who'd last seen her. Perhaps they could figure out why Sally had gone to London, without saying anything.

Rob and Victoria walked via West Port over to the trailer. The new location in Grassmarket was about a fifteen minute walk from the shop. The whisky tasting rooms behind the trailer and other tourist attractions had increased their visibility and profits. Opening the trailer on Saturdays and Sundays meant the business still operated six days a week and The Morrison Street shop could close on Sundays and Mondays.

"Oh, it's awesome," said Victoria as Rob unlocked the red and blue trailer.

"Yeah, this was a good buy. Better than the old stall. You can heat things inside, it's all powered off the generator. We can also move it if we decide to do festivals and things."

"Tell me about Rose?"

"Oh, that's a long story."

"Well how long have you known her?"

"A long time. Why do you want to know?"

"Just being nosy. Sorry if that's not cool."

"I didn't mean to snap. It's just with what happened to her in London, I'm a bit on edge."

"Understandable. She's your buddy as well as your boss. That's right isn't it?"

"Yeah, yeah, that's right. Now let me show you how this all works." Rob was impressed by how quickly Victoria picked everything up. "You've done this before I think?"

"Yeah, something like this, didn't Trixie tell you?"

"I'll bring you the stock and a float around 9.00am Saturday so you can get set up. Then I bring over the prepped muffins for Sunday when you're closing up on Saturday at 6pm."

"Float? Don't you accept card payments?"

"No, not yet. Only at the shop. Most people have cash and, if they don't, there's a free bank machine just over there." He pointed across the street.

"Okay, so Sunday's muffins are day olds?"

"No. That's why the oven and the fridges are here. When we had the stall, the muffins were packed to keep them fresh. Now you get the muffins in their baking cups ready to bake on Sunday."

"Got it. I'll be fine. Do you mind if we finish for today, I can come over tomorrow and run through everything again ready for Saturday. The stall opens at 10am right?"

"The smell of the baking usually means you will open to a queue."

Rob locked the trailer and handed Victoria the keys. "Want a coffee?"

"Thanks but I have some things I need to do, see you tomorrow."

.oOo.

Trixie had just finished cleaning and was about to close the shop when Inspector Hickson knocked on the door. "We're closed," Trixie had called from the back of the shop, not recognising the detective.

"This is Inspector Hickson, can I have a quick word."

Trixie sighed and went over to unlock the door. "Rose isnae back yet. She's still in the hospital in London."

"Yes, I know, I spoke to her and to Anthony. They're coming back tomorrow. That's not why I'm here. It's about Sally. Her mother has reported her missing."

"Right. She said she wis going tae. But it's probably Rob who can help ye more than Ah can. He's the one who saw her that day, the last day she worked Ah mean."

"I will need to speak to him. But what can you tell me. What did you know about Sally?"

"Shall Ah make a tea? I wis just aboot done an' closin' up."

"No tea, thanks. I'm trying to build up a picture of her, who she knew, where she went."

"Tae be honest Ah didnae really know her that' weel. She was nice enough tae work wi', but she was at uni an' only worked the stall, Ah mean the trailer, on the weekend. We didnae hang oot together at all. But Ah wis surprised. She struck me as a wee bit ornery, ye ken. No' someone who would tak off like that."

"And you didn't see her last Saturday?"

"Nae, an' Rob dinnae think there was anything wrong wi' her in the morning, or he would ha' said."

"Thanks. Sorry to have kept you back from closing up."

"Nae problem, but do ye really think she's missin'?"

"She hasn't been seen, or contacted anyone for a week. So it's possible. You might start seeing some news coverage. Her mum is making an appeal. If she does get in touch, please let me know."

"Of course."

"Ah wis goin' tae goo oot wi' ma boyfriend and ask around at some of the clubs tonight."

"Don't do that. It might spook her, especially if Sally doesn't want to be found. Where will I find Rob?"

"Och, ye missed him for the day, Ah can gi' you his phone number though."

"Thanks. I'd like to talk to him before the story goes out on the news."

Trixie locked the door, sent Rob a text forewarning him to expect a phone call from the inspector and then called Graham. "Graham, Ah'm scared. Can ye come get me? I'm leavin' the shop, Ah'll wait at Haymarket Station. It's busy there."

Chapter 15

The doctor taking care of Rose agreed to her leaving the hospital on Friday morning. The tests had all come back positively and the eye doctor was following up with the consultant in Edinburgh.

"You will need to take it easy. And if you get a sudden headache, feel faint or nauseous within the next forty-eight hours, please contact your GP immediately, or go to A&E. I've sent the records up to your GP, but just in case, here's a copy of what you'll need to show them if that happens. The dressing will need to be cleaned and changed on Monday."

"Thanks. I promise, I'll take care."

Anthony produced a hot tea and a pain au chocolat when Rose came out of the ward into the visitors waiting area. "Sorry, I forgot you had asked for one of these yesterday."

Rose beamed and bit into the pastry. "I'm so happy to be going home. I've booked us into first class, I hope you don't mind, it's my treat. Thank you for coming down and everything you've done."

"Rose, you can't splash your money around. I will pay for my ticket. First class makes sense for you though, hopefully you can get some rest."

"Please Anthony. As a thank you. Let's buy some newspapers too for the journey." They bought three different broadsheets, the appeal for Sally was covered in all of them. Rose studied what had been written about the girl.

"Hickson went to see Trixie and spoke to Rob yesterday. I don't think any of us thought anything was wrong until now. I feel horrible, thinking she had stolen some money and that's why she took off."

"Well you don't know that's not right. I mean, she may have done something she regrets and is hiding."

"But not from her mum. I'm sure of that."

"How much money would there be in the float?"

"£250 maybe, £325 on a good day."

"Enough to be tempting then."

"I suppose, but she doesn't seem the type. And she's been with us for a while. If she was short of money, I think she knew me well enough to ask for an advance."

Rose pulled her notebook out of her bag. "Look, this is what's happened since Constance died and I started asking questions."

Anthony looked at the list, and brought out the one he had made at the B&B to compare.

Harry T dead

Donna M dead

Flats in Edinburgh tenancy

Sally*

Andrea Summers threatened

Assault*

"Why the asterisk by Sally and the assault?"

"Because I don't see how Sally or my assault could be connected to the deaths or the property and tenancy issues. The only people who knew I was looking into Constance's death are you, Trixie and Rob, Mike and Marion and Inspector Hickson. I suppose there was also Andrea, William and Mr Mathers after I talked to them though. What if Sally going missing and the assault is connected to something else. What if it's ...?" Her jaw tightened and Anthony could see fear behind the shield over Rose's working eye.

Anthony sat back in his seat, thinking about the murders at the Edinburgh Fringe less than a year before. The mastermind had escaped justice, but would he really risk everything again now, to get back at Rose?

"You thought that too?" Rose said quietly.

"I did, briefly, but it's not his style. He prefers to hide in plain sight, think about how clever he was with disguise. I don't see what he has to gain from coming after you Rose, not now that the dust has settled and he is protected by the big wigs. I don't intend to let that go on forever as I've said to you before. But I haven't poked any bears yet."

"So why was I assaulted, could it be just random?"

Anthony turned Rose's notebook round to face him and tapped on the blank circle she had added. "Who is this?"

"Mr Nobody. Mike hasn't had any luck tracing a son for Harry, so Andrea might have been mistaken. On the other hand, if Harry does have a son and that son found out about Harry's fortune ..."

"Those wills, the ones Mike managed to hack into, how did he know where to find them?"

"I'm not sure, I think he started with Mathers office because he had been the solicitor for all three victims at one point or another, when they were in business together anyway."

"So, they may not be the most recent."

"How?"

"I don't know, I think I'm grasping at straws trying to make sense of everything."

"But you may have something. What will happen now that the deaths are being regarded as suspicious?"

"It will have stopped probate and any monies that may have already changed hands could be frozen, but don't quote me on that. Are you happy to talk to Hickson again when we get back to Edinburgh?"

"About what?"

"Sally, and what happened to you in London."

"She thought I had something to do with Donna, not exactly off to a great start – trust wise - are we."

"You seem to annoy my female counterparts."

"Ah yes, whatever happened to that English DI? Donna? The one who you worked cross border with on the Edinburgh Fringe Murders?" Rose had noticed Donna had seemed sweet on Anthony, or DCI Chatterton, as he had been then.

"Her eyes fell on another younger and more suitable suitor."

"Lucky escape for you, I'd say."

Anthony chuckled. "Well we should speak to Hickson, give her the heads up about Mathers. She may already know about the wills."

"What about Mathers though? I mean, what evidence is there that he's involved in any of this, other than as a solicitor and legal advisor?"

"The man with him. Didn't you say something in a text, about seeing him in Perth?"

"I think so, I can't be totally sure, I got spooked that day, when I thought I was being followed, after I met with Donna. Someone who certainly looks like him had been on the same train as I was, to Perth. Then I thought I saw him again in Perth, then on the platform, waiting for a train going further North. But I really only glimpsed him briefly and as you know," Rose pointed to her eyes. "Not exactly twenty/twenty in that department am I."

Rose gazed out of the window. The landscape changed from rural to city as the train approached York. Rose tried to picture the man's face, what she had actually seen on the journey up to Perth and on the platform. Was it really the same man, or was that her imagination playing tricks, like it had when she thought she was being followed. The train pulled into York Station and the only other passenger in the first class carriage departed. They had been travelling for two hours, her arm was throbbing and she was beginning to feel the effects of her other injuries. They had finished the coffee and sandwiches they bought in London and she wasn't hungry but she nodded when Anthony offered to get some refreshments from the on board cafe.

"Hot chocolate and a pastry if they have any. Thanks."

Eating would help pass the time. What was she missing? She felt like she was finishing a jigsaw where someone else had put some of the edge pieces in the wrong place. What if this hadn't started with Constance being killed? What if she went back to the riding accident, when Constance fell off her horse and the poor animal had to be shot.

"It never hurts to go back in a victim's history," Anthony said when she told him her idea. He watched her making notes and adding to her map, before falling asleep for the remainder of the journey.

Despite Anthony's protests, Rose insisted on going to the shop as soon as the train arrived in Edinburgh. "I promise I'm not going to do anything apart from say hello to Trixie and Rob. I've already texted to say I am coming by to meet this new woman."

"You said that as if she already doesn't come up to your expectations, Rose."

"Oh, did I? Sorry, I didn't mean it like that. It just feels wrong to have hired someone, now that it looks like Sally didn't just run off."

Rose stood outside her shop for a few minutes, watching Trixie serve a customer.

Rob was at the table in the window with a mug of tea. He got up as soon as he saw her. "Welcome home Rose. Oh, your poor face."

"Dinnae fash, as Trixie would say," Rose mumbled, as Rob threw his arms round her and gave her a bear hug.

"Ouch."

"Sorry. We'll fuss over you like there's no tomorrow Rose. And no arguing. Should you really be here?"

"She shouldn't," said Anthony, patting Rob on the back, "but she wouldn't listen to me."

"Rose!" Trixie ran from behind the counter, "I'll get ye a tea."

"No, thanks, we've eaten and drunk loads on the journey. I just wanted to say thank you to you both in person. The shop looks amazing, I can see that you've kept everything going brilliantly. And I wanted to meet Victoria. Isn't she here, I thought it was arranged."

"It was. She went to the trailer earlier, to make sure she felt ready for tomorrow and then texted me. She forgot she had an appointment at 4pm, and sent her apologies."

"OK, that's too bad. I'll go and meet her tomorrow. Have you seen the papers about Sally?"

"Yeah, and it's all over the news. One of the customers suggested we start a reward collection for information. What do you think?"

"Can I suggest that it should be a no." Anthony spoke before Rose could answer.

"Why?" asked Rose.

"Rewards can bring all sorts of idiots out of the woodwork and waste police time following up on the calls."

Rose pulled a face. Still, I think it would show we care. To be honest with you, I'm really uncomfortable that I went ahead and hired Victoria now that it looks like something might have happened to Sally."

"Wait, listen up," Rob said as the local radio interrupted the music for a newsflash. "Missing student Sally Arnold has been found. She has been taken to Edinburgh Royal Infirmary for minor injuries."

"I don't believe it, thank goodness," Rose shouted. "Whatever happened doesn't matter. Let's organise flowers and a taxi home, whatever she needs. I'll call her mum."

"What are we going to do about Victoria?"

"Well, I'll pay her for this weekend of course. Let's see what Sally wants to do. When she can come back to work, hopefully she wants to."

"Rose, Ah think it's time ye went home and rested up. Ye can call Sally's mum frae there. Ah'll organise the flowers once we ken where she is gonnae be staying."

"Thanks Trixie. OK, I'll go, but I will be in tomorrow, just for a bit, see how I do."

Rose gave a familiar formidable look to the group, daring them to argue with her decision.

But rest was not to be. She gasped as she pushed open the door of her flat. "What the …" She turned to Anthony. "Looks like I will be speaking to the Edinburgh police sooner than I hoped."

He put his fingers to his lips and whispered, "Call the police now." He motioned to Rose to wait outside the door. He called out, "Hello." After waiting briefly for a reply he went to the living room. There were books and papers from her files all over the floor, every drawer and cupboard in the kitchen had been turned out. The bedroom was a midden of tangled clothing and laundry. Her bed was stripped and covered in jewellery, make up and creams from her dresser.

"Come on Rose, you can't stay here. Once the police have been, let's get you somewhere safe. You can stay with me if you like."

Rose shook her head. "Thanks, but I really need to be here. I'm not going to let whoever did this drive me out of my home. Not like they did before, which is why I rigged this up." Rose pointed to the top of her wardrobe.

"What am I looking at?"

"Clever isn't it. The camera looks like it's a piece of furniture. There's another one, in the living room. It looks like a plant."

Anthony raised his eyebrows and whistled. "Clever girl. When did you do this?"

"It was Marion's idea. She had someone rig them up for me, after the Edinburgh Fringe murders. They're only on when I'm not home and they're not fancy, so I don't get remote warnings or anything like that. But hopefully they've done their job and we can see whoever was here."

"I'm guessing they're not a professional burglar, it's the sort of thing they would be aware of."

"And that's just it, from the looks of everything nothing has been taken. Not that there's much of value, but it looks like they were looking for something specific. Don't you think?" Rose tried to access the images on her phone but she couldn't make the connection work. "I can't connect to Wi-Fi. I'll check the router, see what's up.' She went back into the bedroom.

"I guess they figured out the cameras after all, the router's switched off. But they had to come in here to do that. There may be an image."

Anthony pulled a face. "Maybe, but ..."

"Yeah, I know, unlikely."

Rose jumped as a uniformed officer appeared behind Anthony. "Sorry, I did knock, but the door was open."

"Yeah, well, this is your crime scene." Rose opened her hands and gestured at the chaos. "It looks like they disabled the cameras I had set up. But you might get lucky."

The young policeman smiled. He was in his early twenties, with red curly hair. "Oh I don't get to do that yet. Someone else is coming and apparently it's an inspector."

"Well aren't I lucky," she rolled her eyes.

"Rose." Anthony's voice retorted. "It may not be Hickson."

"But it is. Hello Rose," said the inspector, treading her way carefully over the piles on the floor. "Fingerprints, although I doubt we'll be lucky and a list of what's missing. Have you checked the door for signs of a break in yet?"

The young policeman flushed and went back into the hall to join another officer.

Inspector Hickson looked at Rose. "My, you are having a run of bad luck aren't you Rose. How are you feeling? You look a little pale."

"I wasn't prepared to find this mess and it's been a long day."

"You can't stay here tonight, we should be finished later, have you somewhere you can go?"

"I've offered, but Rose …"

"No, I get it. Thanks Anthony, I accept. And as far as anything missing, it doesn't seem to be, but I can't really tell in this mess. I had two cameras set up, not all singing all dancing, but whoever came in turned off the Wi-Fi."

"Is it on now, the Wi-Fi?"

"Yes. Rose tried the app on her phone again. There was a shot of a woman in dark clothing entering the living room and going to the wall away from the camera. She was looking through the stack of files on Rose's desk. A man, also in dark clothing with a baseball cap pulled tight over his head and facing down, went straight into the bedroom. Then the image cut out.

"Hmm I doubt we can get anything useful from that. It's interesting there were two of them, we may be lucky with CCTV outside, there's good coverage before you turn into the street. Both of them are slim, I would say in their twenties from the way they move."

"Any idea who they are, Rose?"

"No, no-one I know."

"But you have some interesting friends don't you? Who else has access to the flat?"

Rose counted to three. Hickson's inference was not lost on her, and now wasn't the time to let the woman get under her skin."Rob has a spare set of keys and there is a spare set at the shop. My downstairs neighbour, in case of an emergency, that's all."

"I'll need to speak to the other key holders and check if the ones at the shop are still there."

"When did you travel to Bristol?"

"A week ago, I caught the train last Friday."

"We don't know when. It could have happened before or after your assault in London? There's no date or time on the recording, let's hope there's CCTV"

Rose shrugged. "My rig up is not state of the art. Do you think the assault and this are connected."

"What I think Rose is that you should keep your head down, run your shop and stay out of matters that don't concern you."

"Now look here, I ..."

"Rose, Inspector Hickson is just doing her job." Anthony's eye's flashed a warning as he spoke.

"Quite right DCI, sorry, Mr Chatterton." Inspector Hickson corrected herself, "Thank you. Someone will be in touch. We'll give you a crime number for insurance and we'll need to take a statement. Can you come to the station tomorrow sometime, or Monday?"

"Yes, of course."

"Well, try and get some sleep. You look like you could use it."

Rose and Anthony made their way back downstairs. Rose only just managed to keep her opinion about the inspector contained until they reached the pavement. "That bloody woman. Who does she think she is!"

"I know, but she was right about one thing Rose, you look shattered. Let's go to mine and I'll order in whatever you fancy."

Chapter 16

Trixie had pulled out all the stops and started baking at 5am on Saturday morning to make sure everything was ready for the shop and the trailer. She arranged a car to drive Sally to her mother's house in Seaton Sands. Rob had collected the baking and was cycling over to the infirmary with flowers and a box of fresh muffins for Sally, before heading back over to the trailer to meet Victoria.

'Thanks Rob, I'm sure I'll be fine by next weekend. I really don't know what happened. I don't do drugs, or drink that much. The police are coming to see me again later, at mum's.'

'Just take care and get better. Rose will probably call you later too. You know about what happened to her?'

'Yeah, I can't believe it. Do you think what happened to me and to her are connected somehow?'

'Rose does, she didn't stop texting me last night, I think she was driving Anthony mad with all her questions. She did ask me to show you this.' Rob pulled up the picture of the young man with Mathers Rose had taken in London. 'Do you remember seeing him at all?'

Sally leaned forward and nodded. "He was with Victoria, he's her brother."

"You met Victoria? When?"

"Last Saturday. They said they were friends with Rose, they wanted to give her a surprise."

"Oh my God. Sally I need to get hold of Rose."

Sally looked down at her phone and frowned.

"What is it?" Rob asked.

"Rose thought I'd stolen the float. There's a text." Sally showed Rob her phone screen. .

"Yeah, I guess we all thought you'd just taken off. Your flatmate said you'd gone to London."

"There also appears to be a text on my phone to my flatmate. But I'm sure I didn't write it. Why would I go to London?"

"Sorry Sally. None of us thought it was like you. You've got to believe that."

"Thanks, I wish I could remember what happened. I know how it must have looked. Did you find the float?"

"Nope. The trailer was locked, keys were gone along with the cash. You were nowhere in sight."

"What time was that?"

"Oh, about 5.30pm, the usual time I come over, but the woman on the soap stall said she thought she had seen you lock up around 4pm."

"I think that's right, it was early when they persuaded me to close up. I'm so sorry."

"I'd better get over to the trailer, see you soon, and I mean it, Sally, anything you need. Please tell the police what you have just told me. It's really important they know as soon as possible."

Heading back down to the bike Rob shot a quick text to Trixie and Rose.

OK somethings weird. Sally met Victoria and the man Rose took a picture of in London. She doesn't know what happened to her, but I think they may be behind why she disappeared. Who the hell is Victoria? I'm heading to the trailer now to have it out with her.

.oOo.

Rose wrinkled her nose as she read the text She looked at the notebook and added Sally to the map, with an arrow joining her to the man in the photograph and a question mark. Then sent Rob a text.

Be really careful Rob. I'll tell Anthony and call Inspector Hickson.

She cast her mind back to meeting Donna in Perth. Showing her the photograph of her with the Canadian family had spooked her, but why?

Anthony arrived with a steaming mug of tea and a plate of hot buttered toast and jam. "Morning Rose. I heard you were up, hungry?"

"Yes, thanks. And I'm sorry if I grilled you last night."

'It's OK, I think you might have driven Mike and Rob a bit crazy with all the texting. Your brain was wired."

"I get like that. Look, is there any chance we could find out what the substance that they found in Harry, Constance and Donna's body is?"

"I doubt it. Not now all the deaths are an official murder investigation."

"And do you think they'll solve what happened?"

"I hope so, they'll do what they can. What's worrying me is how you have been drawn into it. I don't mean just the hunches you had but the attack, Sally going missing. It feels personal Rose."

"I know. And it is. She showed him Rob's text about Sally knowing Victoria and saying the man from London was her brother. We need to call Hickson and let her know. What if what happened to Sally was because of me somehow? What else are they capable of? Rob has told Sally to tell the police as soon as possible."

Rose left the inspector a message about what she had just found out and let her know Rob was on his way to meet Victoria at the trailer.

"Did I tell you about the dreams I've been having, about Troy?"

"No."

Rose described the dreams to Anthony, "It feels like he's haunting me."

"He's locked up. He will be for years. Perhaps you need to talk to the counsellor again."

"Maybe. But right now, I want to talk to the vet who shot Constance's horse at the event. Mike has located him, although he's retired now. Well, lost his license to practise. He also had some abuse after the incident and the man who ran the livery where the horse was from lost his business. Something about toxins in the food."

Rose showed Anthony the newspaper articles Mike had sent her links for, "What did we do before the internet?"

"Methodical research. It took longer, that's for sure." Anthony studied the newspaper articles and made some notes.

"I've got a phone number for the vet, but I'd really like to speak to him in person. Do you fancy a trip to Stirling?"

"You're supposed to be resting. My car is in for servicing, and it's not going to be ready until Monday. But I can see keeping you in isn't an option. Sure, I'll come with you. I'll make up some big muckles to take with us."

"Careful you'll be talking like Trixie soon. A big veggie muckle would be great."

Rose picked up her phone to text Mike when a call from Rob came in.

"There's no one at the trailer and I talked to the soap lady again. She thinks Victoria and that man, who according to Sally is Victoria's brother, were hanging around a couple of times. The police have already spoken to Sally."

"Victoria and that man are brother and sister?"

"Yep.'"

"And they kidnapped Sally?"

"Looks like it Rose. She really had Trixie and I fooled. Smooth, charming, funny. Sorry."

"How on earth would you even begin to think she wasn't who she seemed. It was weird though, how she appeared so quickly to apply for Sally's job."

"Yeah and something else. When we were in the kitchen talking about Sally, she told us a story about a time she had run away. Told us Sally would be fine."

"Because she knew she would. How sick. But at least they didn't really hurt Sally, apart from … no forget that they did really hurt her. They're clearly pretty dark human beings."

"Remind you of anyone? Look I'm heading back to the shop to help Trixie. The trailer is obviously going to have to stay closed this weekend Rose. Inspector Hickson is going to come over to the shop to talk to me this afternoon."

'No problem. And thank you Rob. A least …"

"What Rose?"

"Nothing, I'm probably imagining things, could it have been Victoria and her brother who broke into my flat?"

"Could have, maybe that's why she wanted to work here."

Rose got herself ready. She was still sore and achy, but her head was clearer. After speaking to Rob and learning about what had happened to Sally she had the beginnings of an idea, but she didn't dare speak it out loud in case it vaporised before she had grasped it properly.

.oOo.

Anthony's flat was sparse and uncluttered. The bedroom she had slept in was freshly painted but the walls were bare apart from the two bookcases either side of the window. She looked at the books. There was a lot of nonfiction about police work, the history of policing, poisons and legal tombs. His taste in fiction tended towards the classics, Steinbeck, Joyce, Dickens, and others and a surprising collection of books of poetry by Mary Oliver, Percy Bysshe Shelley, and Ted Hughes. The other book case was filled with crime fiction. The two upper shelves were filled with titles by Agatha Christie, Ruth Rendell, PD James and Dorothy L Sayers. Various American crime writers, including John Grisham and Patricia Cornwell, filled the lower shelves.

"Reading is a bit of a busman's holiday for you then Anthony?" Rose came out of the kitchen holding a book.

"Ah, yes 'The Art Of Poison', that's a good read," he chuckled looking at the book.

"I thought it might be useful for research, mind if we take it?"

"Sure, why not. Sandwiches are ready, shall we go?"

Anthony's flat was in the north of the city, on the edge of Stockbridge. The area had become trendy and vibrant as the once run-down Georgian streets were restored and done up. Cafes and arts events gave it a bohemian vibe. An arts market, on the corner of the crescent where Anthony lived, was in full swing as they left the flat.

"Two buses and a train ride, are you sure you're up to it?" Anthony asked Rose as they walked towards the bus stop.

"Oh yes. It's so nice to be in the fresh air and doing something. That hospital bed reminded me how far I had come from my other lifestyle, the one that almost killed me. I need it."

Settled on the train to Stirling, Rose opened the book. She started reading about noxious herbs and plants that can be found anywhere. She tapped the page on yew.

"If a horse ingests this, they'll become really sick, they could die quite quickly. But if you didn't want to kill the animal, just make it feel ill, or unbalanced, and you knew what you were doing dose wise ..." Rose read from the book. "It will cause muscle trembling, incoordination, nervousness, difficulty breathing, slow heart rate. The newspaper reports said the horse looked unstable when she made it take the jump."

Anthony read the page.

'It's also highly dangerous for humans. Could be the common toxin the lab reported finding in Constance, Harry and Donna.'

'I don't think so, well I'm not a chemist, but I think the symptoms would have made the pathologist suspicious, when they first examined Constance I mean. It looks like there would be symptoms, although as she had been dead for a while, maybe not.''

Rose closed the book and looked out of the window at the passing countryside. They had just passed through Falkirk, the train would arrive in Stirling in the next ten minutes. According to Mike's research, the vet who had shot the horse after the fall lived in the Riverside area of Stirling.

"Odd don't you think, for a vet to move into a city?"

"Well people could say that about me. A retired policeman from London, finally settling in Edinburgh. And Stirling has lots of easy access to nature."

"True, not that I know it well."

The weather, as it often does in Scotland, had changed from bright blue skies to a torrential downpour as they alighted the train. "It's not far, but I think we'd better get a taxi," said Rose.

"Do we know he's even going to be home?"

"No, but if he isn't we can wait close by.. Mike's information suggested he wasn't that well, so he won't be far."

The taxi ride was less than five minutes from the station. The 19th century stone building had been converted into flats and two young women with backpacks were leaving just as Rose and Anthony arrived. They were talking to an older man who was putting out some rubbish.

"Dr Graham?" Rose asked

The man looked at Rose, "Just plain Mr, but yes Graham is right. Do I know you?" He looked at Rose carefully. She realised she must look a bit of a fright with the head dressing and the eye shield.

"No, but I would really appreciate talking to you for a bit, if that's alright. It's about one of my customers - I have a shop in Edinburgh- she died earlier this year."

Mr Graham put his hand up. "No, sorry I can't help you. Good day." He turned and walked quickly back towards the door at the side of the house.

Rose followed him, "Please, I really think you might be able to help. You know who I'm talking about don't you."

The man's complexion turned ashen, beads of perspiration started to appear on his forehead. "Yes, yes I know. She's the reason I ended up in this dump."

Rose looked around at the building. A young man was fixing a bike in the overgrown back garden. The property wasn't well cared for, and the outside badly needed a coat of exterior paint.

"Living with students, at my age. "The man shook his head.

"I'm sorry, I didn't mean to upset you, but perhaps if we can talk about what happened, what you know, it might help."

"I'm glad she's dead."

"Really? You know that she wasn't found for weeks afterwards."

"You don't understand."

"But if you talked to me it would help me to understand."

"Who is that?" He nodded his head towards Anthony.

"He's a retired policeman. He's helping me find out why Constance Brown was murdered."

"Murdered? I thought she'd just died."

"No, apparently not."

The man sighed and cocked his head, studying Rose again. "You look like you've been in the wars, what happened?"

"Tell you mine if you tell me yours ...?" Rose attempted humour to break the stalemate.

"Alright. Come away in, both of you. It's a story alright."

The flat was not as dismal on the inside. The walls were adorned with framed photographs of cattle, sheep and horses. There were several framed documents over the fireplace and trophy cups and plaques were on display in a glass fronted cabinet.

Rose and Anthony settled on a large brown sofa which despite its age was comfortably squishy. The rest of the furniture had also seen better days. Mr Graham hovered. "Would you like a cup of tea, or coffee? I don't drink, I'm afraid."

"And it would be way too early. Coffee if it's not a bother," said Rose. "Can I help?"

"No, I can manage." He shuffled out of the room and returned with three mugs on a tray and a plate of shortbread.

"Beautiful pictures, did you take them?" Rose asked.

"Everything here represents who I used to be, my former life."

"I've had one of those, so has Anthony."

"Well, mine wasn't as dramatic a change as Rose had. I'm rather boring in comparison"

Rose shook her head, "Not True at all."

There was an awkward silence as the three of them sipped the hot coffee and dunked the shortbread.

"So, Constance was murdered?" He shook his head. "She was always one for a bit of the drama, but murder. Are you sure? I don't know how I can help. I haven't seen the woman since ..."

"I'm interested in the accident. The horse, what you think happened. And why there was such a furore afterwards. You said she liked drama, what did you mean?"

"Constance was a stunning young woman, and an amazing rider. She could captivate a room just by walking into it. I met her when I was newly qualified but I was beginning to build a good reputation. I wanted to establish myself as specialising in horses. I worked with cattle too, but eventually my practice did become exclusively horses. I was also a rider and played polo." He pointed to the cabinet with the cups. "Polo didn't make me popular in veterinary circles, but Constance and Harry didn't have a problem with it. When Constance asked me to work with her horses and later, with the charity she started, I was flattered."

"You got to know her well," Anthony said.

"Yes and no. I knew her professionally as her veterinary advisor, I assessed any horses she bought and rode, I even travelled with her to the Olympics. But she kept me in my place when it came to social gatherings or discussing anything other than horses."

"Tell me about the event she took part in, the charity event. Were you on duty as the vet that day?"

"No. The organisers had their own team of vets, but I was there. I saw the horse before the event and I mentioned to Geoff, he was the owner of the livery where Jet was housed, that the horse seemed unsteady, a little wound up. He spoke to a young woman he'd brought with him one of his stable hands, and reassured me that everything was alright. But of course, as it turned out, it was far from alright. I knew as soon as the horse refused the jump that Constance should have taken him off the course, something was wrong, it was the way he refused it. His foreleg looked weak from where I was watching. When she jumped him, he fell and rolled onto her. She was badly injured. She was actually very lucky to survive – let alone walk again. "

"But it was you that put the horse down, is that right?"

"Yes. And that decision got me barred from practising as a vet."

"Why not leave the decision to the organisers?"

"Geoff asked me to help the horse. The organisers were taking forever to make a decision and the poor animal was in so much pain. The whole rotten business cost Geoff too. After, the rumours started."

"What rumours?"

"That Jet had had access to yew. The other owners removed their horses from his care, and he lost his business. Geoff tried to fight it, there was no yew on his property or nearby, but it was hopeless. I went to the auction to support Geoff. The auction was run by a London solicitor for some reason."

164

"Do you remember his name?"

"No, but I could give you a number for Geoff. We still keep in touch. He would know."

"Do you have any photographs of the day?"

"I do. I keep meaning to get rid, but ..." He shrugged and got up to walk over to the cabinet. As he opened one of the cupboards underneath the display Rose saw it was full of photograph albums, envelopes, and folded sheets of newspaper. The photographs of the event were in a brown envelope. There were several of Jet, one of Constance Brown and Harry with Jet, and a shot of the horsebox, with a young woman leading the horse out. In the background and almost out of shot was a young man. Rose peered at the picture more closely. Pointing at the photograph she turned to Anthony. "I can't be a hundred percent sure, but I think that's the man I saw with Mathers in London, who we now think he's Victoria's brother?'

Anthony leaned in to look. "Yes, I think it is."

"What is it?" Mr Graham asked.

"This man, do you know who he is, why was he there, do you know?"

"No idea, but I did see him later with the stable hand. They seemed to know each other quite well. They were both American I think."

Rose looked at Anthony. "I wonder ..."

"What is it?"

"Not sure but something's just clicked. Back to Perth. There was a girl in the waiting room at the station, she was wearing a Canadian button on her coat. The same button that the man, this man, I think I saw on the train and in London was wearing."

"Not sure I get it what you're connecting together Rose,"' Anthony said.

"Nor do I yet. Do you mind if I take a picture of this photo, I want to send it to someone?"

"It's fine, if it helps you."

"Thanks.' Rose turned to Anthony, 'I'll send the picture to Rob, maybe this girl is Victoria. So the question is, why is she working at the stable with the same horse that Constance rode?"

Rose sent a copy of the picture to Rob. *Is this Victoria?*
Yes, that's her. With the same man!

Rose showed Anthony the text. 'Thanks Mr Graham. This has been really helpful.'

"My name's Tim. It's OK, I don't get many visitors, my social skills are a bit short these days."

They shook hands. Anthony put his hand on Rose's shoulder, as they left the building. "Your instincts Rose, are spot on. If we hadn't gone to see him, I doubt we'd have ever found out about that photograph."

"Something else to tell Hickson. I hope she's going to start warming up towards me."

.oOo.

"Expect what?" Rose said as she and Anthony came into the shop, overhearing the tail end of a conversation between Rob and Trixie. "Looks like you both sold everything there was to sell today."

"Aye, it's been busy. How are ye? Where di ye find that picture of Victoria and the horse?"

Rose turned to Anthony. 'Shall we fill them in now, or keep them guessing?

"I also sent the photograph to Mike." Rose held up her phone and showed Trixie and Rob the picture of the woman leading the horse out of the horse box. "I also called Geoff who used to run the stables before the accident ruined him. And he told me that the woman who worked for him at the stables – the one we know as Victoria – he knew her as 'Amy'."

Anthony continued, "Mike found a picture of someone who looks like the same stable hand, but her hair is different too. According to the caption she was called Joanna and was from Musselburgh, which is where Harry Turnbull lived."

"Shall I make tea?' asked Rob."

"No, unless you two have plans, I'd like us all to have dinner together, my treat. I have some news that I want to share with you. Noting about murders or puzzles or anything bad. Some really good news! The new pizzeria has a great menu, let's go there. Then I'll go back and clean up the flat. The police are all finished.'

'But there's ...'

"Lots to talk about and I for one am famished.

Chapter 17

The new pizzeria was busy with locals and tourists. Rose waved and smiled at several of her shop's customers, following the server to a table at the back of the room. The upcycled wooden chairs and tables were painted red, blue or yellow. Each table had a little candle holder in the shape of a Gondola and a white candle. The colours of the furniture contrasted with the whitewashed walls which set off the black and white photographs of Italian movie stars, singers and famous landmarks of Rome, Florence and Venice. Everyone had just settled down at the table when Rose felt her phone vibrate in her pocket. "Kay, we're about to have dinner, can I call you back?"

"I'm so sorry Rose, has the care home managed to get through to you?"

"No. I didn't realise I had my phone on silent. Is everything alright? Is it Dad …?"

"Rose, I'm so sorry. I hate giving you the news on the phone, but I knew you'd want to know as soon as possible, your dad passed away in his sleep this afternoon. The manager tried to call you, she tried several times but she couldn't get through. So she called me." Rose brought the phone down onto the table, and sat staring into the device.

"Wit is it Rose? Wha's happened," Trixie leaned across the table. Rose shook her head and looked around at her friends, "He's gone," she whispered. "Dad's gone."

Rob lifted the phone from Rose, he could hear Kay's voice calling her name. "Kay, it's Rob. Anthony and Trixie are here too. We'll take care of Rose right now and call you back. She'll want to come down."

"Yes, and she can stay with me. Just let me know what arrangements she wants put in place and when she's coming."

Rob put the phone on the table and tried to cradle Rose's still and silent body in his arms. "Come on Rose, let it out, whatever you need to do."

Rose pushed him away and got up slowly from the table. Ignoring the cacophony of voices from Trixie, Anthony and Rob, calling her name, pleading with her to wait, she ran out of the restaurant.

"I'll go after her," said Rob.

Anthony and Trixie stared after him, and watched as he caught Rose outside of the restaurant, pulling her into him. She struggled, then allowed her body to go limp. Her face contorted and she began to wail.

"Och, thank goodness," Trixie turned to Anthony.

"After everything else, it seems so cruel." Anthony picked up Rose's phone from the table. "I'll take her back to my place, she can't go to her flat after this, the place still needs cleaning and sorting from the break in."

Trixie shook her head, "Knowing Rose, Ah think she'll want to go straight to Bristol. I doubt we'd be able to convince her to stay."

Anthony pulled up the train timetable on his phone and then checked flights. "She'll not be able to. The next train will take over 11 hours, and she'll be stuck overnight. She won't get to the airport in time for the last flight. There's no available morning flight on Sunday, until 17.15pm, and the 08.00 train arrives sooner, so that's probably the better option."

"OK, well let's suggest that. Look, they're coming back in."

Rose was pale, moving as if she was carrying a huge load, her shoulders hunched over. She flopped into a chair. "I can't eat, but you all should. Is it too late to …"

Catching her thought Trixie replied, "Tonight, aye Rose, but the morrow, there's a train first thing. Anthony just looked at the options. Ah can go an' fetch ye a bag wi some things fer ye tae tak?"

"Dad had sorted everything. The care home and the solicitor know what to do, who to contact." Rose leaned over the table and put her head on her arms. "I can't think, I just want not to have to think about anything anymore."

Anthony, Rob and Trixie exchanged glances. No-one wanted to eat, Rose's hopelessness was painful.

.oOo.

It was after ten by the time Rose was finally settled in the spare room at Anthony's. Trixie went to Rose's flat with Rob and put together a bag for Rose while Rob tidied up as best he could, making up her bed and stacking the papers.

Then made their way over to Anthony's in a taxi. Rob called Kay back and she urged them not to push Rose into any decision. "Everything at this end is taken care of. The cremation will be on Friday, so there's lots of time between now and then for her to be able to travel. I would offer to come up and bring her back, but we are still short staffed at the hospital."

Anthony suggested he travel with Rose. Trixie and Rob would need to manage the shop. The three of them sat in silence as they each thought about what had just happened.

"Rose was going to tell us something before Kay called. Do you know what it is Anthony?"

"No idea."

"Did Victoria show you any identification when you took her on?"

Trixie looked down and started biting her lip. "Ye know, she had references an' a really nice manner, I didnae think tae ask her. She told me she was eligible to work in the UK, that she had a British passport. Ah should hae' checked."

"You and me both," said Rob.

"Can I suggest you both go and get a good night's sleep. Stop worrying about what you didn't do, it won't help. I'll talk to the inspector without dropping Mike in it. I'm not at all sure the software he's using is legal. We need to find out who this woman is, and what she's up to."

Anthony set about making his own version of Rose's map when the others left, adding Victoria's name to the group of people he and Rose had identified on their journey back from London, linking her to the man with Mathers and Harry Turnbull and adding a question mark. He read through the note's he had taken after the evening he and Rose had gone to look at Constance's building. The neighbour had told Rose she had heard or seen an argument between Constance and a young American couple. He looked at the photograph Rose had taken at the vet's flat. Were these the same people?

The vet, Tim, said they sounded American, but what if they had been Canadian? His instinct told him it was worth following up with the neighbour, to see if she recognised the photograph of the woman who had pretended to be Victoria. He was about to go to bed when he heard Rose getting up and being sick in the bathroom.

He waited for her to go back to the bedroom and took her a glass of water.

"How are you? Sorry, that was a stupid question."

"It's okay, I just feel numb. But I had another one of those dreams about Troy shooting horses. Every time I think of that man I feel sick and sometimes, well sometimes I am, literally."

"I'm going to speak to Hickson, see if the woman in the photograph has come up in any of her investigations."

"Don't tell her about Mike's equipment, please."

"I won't I already figured that out. And I don't want to know how or why he's got such a sophisticated programme."

Rose smiled. "There'll be a good reason, but probably best if we don't ask what it is."

"See you in the morning. If you can't sleep, you can wake me, or plough through the books. Maybe some light fiction will help take your mind off …"

"Dad dying," Rose completed the awkward sentence. "I have some music on my phone. My AA sponsor suggested some soothing tracks last time I was struggling. I'll be okay. Thanks for everything you've done. I called Kay and let her know I would go down on Wednesday."

"I can come with you."

"Thanks, but I'll be fine. Goodnight."

Anthony paused, then closed the door, relieved she seemed calmer.

.oOo.

The following morning Inspector Hickson was enthusiastic about the information Anthony shared with her. He was glad she appeared less frosty than she had been towards Rose.

"Thanks, yes, I appreciate you telling me about the photographs. Will Rose still be able to come down to the station and give her statement about the break in today? I'm sorry about her father. Let me know what time and I'll arrange to be here. It's already one of those days, and it's only just after nine. Another Monday. Do you miss it?"

"Sometimes. But not Monday's, especially after a busy weekend. I'll give you a call when Rose wakes up."

"She's had a tough couple of weeks. She's fortunate she has friends like you."

"Thanks," the inspector's words reminded him of the dinner party on Rose's birthday, his discussion with Marion. Rose wasn't fortunate in so many ways, but she did bring people together. Her open heart and generous nature were what had made her shop so successful. Why people liked going there. And now, more than ever she'd need her tribe, as she called her friends. He was surprised to find himself hoping he was a tribe member too, as he set about making them both breakfast.

Rose chewed absently on a bit of toast. "I need to get this dressing changed today, and see the doc about whether I still need to wear this shield. It seems so much better now it's not swollen."

Anthony looked at her. Her eye did look a lot better and the bruises on her face had faded. But she looked exhausted.

"Did you sleep at all?"

"On and off. So what's the plan? Police station for my statement and then hospital? I need to keep busy today."

"Alright. Look, I told Inspector Hickson about the photograph from the vet. She wants to see it. I'd also like to go and talk to Constance Brown's neighbour."

"What do you want to see the neighbour about?"

"Remember she said she had heard an argument, a young couple, she thought they were American. Well Victoria told Trixie she was Canadian?"

"Right. So, you think the neighbour might recognise the photograph? Mind if I come too."

Anthony laughed. "Well as you started this whole thing, I would expect nothing less."

"Good, for a moment there I thought we'd swapped roles. Let's go there first, then to the police. Now we're sharing information with Hickson, the more we have to tell her, the better."

The garage called to let Anthony know his car was ready. With the different locations they needed to get to he thought driving would be a better option. Rose was quiet, lost in her own thoughts, while they drove over to Morningside.

The neighbour fussed when she opened the door and saw Rose's injuries.

"Honestly I'm really doing alright, and this is all healing. I've no idea who did it, a random mugging." Rose looked across at Anthony, he nodded. It was best not to suggest that whoever attacked Rose might be connected to what was happening with the property. "I'm sorry I didn't get the chance to talk to the solicitor. Can I show you a photograph? We were wondering if you recognise the people in it? Could they be the same people you heard arguing with Constance before she had the accident? The woman may have had a different hairstyle."

Rose held up her phone and made the picture as bright as possible, zooming in on the young woman and the man in the background.

"I'm not sure, it was a long time ago and they were outside the window. They had their backs to me. I'm sorry."

"You told me they sounded American, could they have been Canadian?"

She shrugged. "I haven't travelled that much, so I probably wouldn't know the difference. But he definitely had an accent from somewhere on the North American continent."

"Thanks. I'm sorry again that I haven't been any help regarding the lease. I hope you manage to find somewhere."

"Och, it'll all be fine. Janice, my daughter is busy at it everyday. You take care o' yersel' and get better."

Rose was just about to close the door of the car when the young woman they had met last time came out. "Hello again."

"Oh, hello. You're back. Are you moving in?"

"No. We came over to see the lady downstairs. But hey, do you mind me asking, have you ever seen either of these people before, maybe talking to Constance?"

The girl looked at the phone and nodded. "Yes, yes, they were here a long time ago. I only remember because they were having a big row, right here in the garden. This man pushed Constance. Her friend - the older man who used to visit - had to stop her from falling over. It was very shocking. We were coming back from the park and had to wait here on the street. Then the younger ones left and drove off."

"Do you remember what they were driving?"

She shook her head. "No, sorry. Big car though, like that one." She pointed to an SUV parked further down the street.

Anthony looked up and down the street, hoping to spot a CCTV camera. But he was out of luck.

"Thanks," said Rose. "Will you be moving or staying with the rents all going up?"

"We're hoping to stay. But ...," she opened her hands and shrugged.

"OK, well good luck."

Rose leaned over and pulled her notebook out of her bag. "Who the devil are these two? They had an argument with Constance in March, a month before the riding accident, he knew Mathers, she worked for Harry Turnbull and, for some reason, she tried to work for me. I wonder when she started working with the horse."

Rose tapped the face of the woman with the horse in the photograph on her phone. "I think we should go to Musselburgh, see if we can find anyone who met her, maybe they saw her together with him."

"Rose, you're supposed to be ..." Anthony saw from the expression of Rose's face that trying to dissuade her was hopeless. If he didn't go with her to Musselburgh, she'd no doubt go on her own.

"The dressing can wait until later, the hospital will be quieter then anyway."

"And your eye? I thought the eye clinic was only open until 2pm?"

"It's fine, they just said to have someone check it was healing, which it is. I have an appointment with the specialist next week. It can wait until then."

"Won't you be staying in Bristol?"

"Not after the service. On Wednesday I'll collect everything from the care home, see the solicitor and sign whatever needs to be signed. Then after the service on Friday morning, I'll come straight back. I can't face going to the house yet."

"Fair enough, Police and then Musselburgh?"

"Drive on James, drive on."

Making her statement didn't take long but Inspector Hickson had been called out and couldn't get back to the police station. It was after 1pm by the time they arrived in Musselburgh.

Harry's house was a large detached Victorian stone villa. The area was full of large homes and walled or gated properties. Harry's was by no means the grandest, but it was beautiful. Reminiscent of a different time, when families would have had daily or live-in staff. The villa was close to the town, on the East side of the old Fisherrow Harbour, facing towards the River Esk and the sand dunes.

"Where do you want to start, Rose?"

"I was thinking of a neighbour. That terrace is the closest to Harry's, although it's not exactly next door. The grounds around the villa are huge."

"It's a semi-retired community, so we might get lucky with a window watcher living on the terrace."

"There's one, possibly," Rose pointed to a large window with a man's face peering out of it. "It might be better if you go ask him, I think I look a bit scary with the eye shield and bandages and this cast."

Rose watched Anthony cross the road towards the terrace and knock on the door. He tried the window watcher, and several others, but his blank face told Rose that he'd had no luck. "Shall we have some lunch? There's a couple of cafe's on the corner."

"Yeah, and if we're lucky, she might have gone to one of the cafe's to meet him, whoever he is."

Anthony was locking up the car when he spotted the man coming out of Harry's front door. "Rose, look around, back over at the villa."

"That's William Summers."

Chapter 18

They watched William leave the grounds of the villa and walk up the hill, into the same cafe where Rose and Anthony planned to have lunch. Following discretely from the other side of the road they saw him take a seat at a corner table by the window. He placed his coat and a rucksack on two chairs at the same table. "It's too small for us to eat in there without him seeing us." Rose said.

"He doesn't know me. I'll go in. Why don't you go to the cafe opposite, I can text you. From the way he's arranged the chairs, It looks like he's meeting someone."

Rose agreed to the plan. "I can also ask them if they have seen Victoria."

The cafe was busy. To avoid sitting too close to William's table Anthony decided to share a table with a young father trying to feed an active toddler in a high chair in the middle of the room. "Sorry, he's a bit messy," apologised the young father, mopping up the spillage.

"No bother at all," said Anthony. He wasn't particularly drawn to children, but this one with a mop of curly red hair had given him a broad grin when he sat down. Anthony waved. The child waved back. He realised the game was a perfect camouflage, as two others arrived to sit down with William Summers. Anthony raised his eyebrows when he realised who they were. Continuing to engage with the toddler, Anthony had a good view of the seated trio. He texted Rose.

Victoria and her brother, the man you saw with Mathers are here.

OMG!

Exactly

The younger man's voice was loud, as he ordered coffee and sandwiches, his accent was definitely North American. He told the server to bring their drinks and food orders for take away.

Be ready to leave. Looks like they aren't staying here.

Giving the toddler a final wave and gulping down the coffee he had ordered, Anthony left the cafe ahead of the group. He signalled to Rose when she appeared outside the cafe opposite to wait around the corner and crossed the road to join her. "They won't notice us from here, but we can see where they are going."

Rose pointed to a blue SUV parked opposite the cafe.

"If that's theirs and they drive off, we've no chance, my car is back down the hill.

But the trio didn't get into the SUV when they left the cafe. They walked back down the hill towards Harry's house. "Why are they carrying four coffee's?" asked Rose.

"Good question. It's probably best if we sit in the car and watch, see if we can observe anything going on inside, but the house is set back from the road, so I doubt it. I'll let Hickson know we've spotted them. Hopefully they can send a car to talk to Victoria and her brother - if he is her brother - regarding Sally."

Anthony finished leaving a message for Inspector Hickson when a mini cab pulled up just as the group arrived at the house. A tall thin man got out. He was wearing a black track suit and a hoodie. "What's he doing here?"

"Who Rose, do you know him?"

"I could swear I do. I'm almost sure it's Stuart Dunphy, a close friend of Troy's and no friend of mine."

"You think they're still in touch?"

"Oh yeah. They were pretty tight. Stuart's got away with all sorts over the years. He flies right under the radar. I know he would have enjoyed helping Troy put me in prison."

She pulled out her camera and took a video as the group greeted the other man and they went into the house. But everybody had their back to her by then. She took a picture of the mini cab driver as he drove past. At least we might be able to find out the name he used, if it isn't Stuart I mean. Hickson could find out, couldn't she? Unless you fancy …"

"No Rose, I've already been mistaken for a policeman by the doorman in Sloane Street. I should have disabused him, but I didn't. Pretending to be a policeman sails a bit too close to the wind for me. I'm sorry."

"I get it. Mind if I try?"

"I can't stop you Rose. Go ahead."

"I'll do it out of earshot, I don't want to make you uncomfortable." But Rose had no luck with the taxi service, despite her story that she was trying to return something to the man who had ordered the taxi, the office wouldn't confirm or deny the name of the passenger.

They had been sitting in the car for over two hours before anyone came out. First William Summers with the man Rose thought was Stuart. The younger pair followed them. But when they got to the gate they separated. Rose took some pictures through the car window.

"Who do we follow?"

Anthony pointed up the hill towards the SUV. "Looks like you were right about the vehicle. Let's see where they're going."

"OK. I'm going to text Mike and Marion, see if they can find out anything about Stuart. Maybe the last time Stuart saw Troy at the prison. One of them will probably have a mate somewhere who'll be able to help."

"Heavens to Betsy, Rose, don't tell me these things!"

The SUV made its way out of Musselburgh with Anthony driving cautiously on its tail. But as soon as the car turned off the road, towards Edinburgh, he was stopped by a traffic light and lost sight of the SUV.

"Where did they go?"

"They must have taken a side road. Sorry I couldn't risk running the light."

"At least you gave Hickson the registration Marion said Mike was going to help with the visiting orders at the prison."

"How did you meet this Stuart?"

"He came to Troy's house a lot. Rob will remember him. Drove flashy cars, and always had too much cash if you know what I mean. He gave me the creeps, but I think Troy enjoyed the tension."

Anthony nodded. "He sounds like a lovely piece of work."

"You'd be shocked if you knew what I put up with back then."

Anthony sighed. As a policeman, he could easily imagine what Rose had to put up with. He had seen lots of cases of abuse that didn't use physical force to control someone. He looked across at her and winced at how vulnerable she looked with the dressing on her head and the eye shield. "Let's get you to the hospital. At least they can change that dressing and look you over. "I have just remembered something."

"What is it?"

"It was seeing Stuart in that black hoodie. The man who attacked me in Sloane Street, was wearing a black tracksuit and hoodie. When he went to kick me, there was a logo on the bottom of the trouser, a red triangle."

"I'm not sure that's going to help the police much, I'm sorry, there must be hundreds of men in outfits like that with brands and logos."

"Yeah, but I think that brand is fairly unique - expensive I mean."

Rose typed a short text to Rob and attached the photo

It's been a few years Rose, but it could be Stuart. Where are you?

Musselburgh. We've seen Victoria and the man who was with Mathers in London. They've all been at Harry Turnbull's House together.

Anthony with you?

Yes, of course. He won't let me out of his sight.

Good. Stay safe and close to him. BTW Trixie had a text from Sally, she's not coming back to work.

Oh too bad. I'll try and call her. Let her know I understand.

"How far away are we from Seaton Sands? Wondering if we could see Sally at her mum's?" Rose mused.

"I don't think we should roll up unannounced. And I'd really like you to get seen at the hospital today, you told the doctor in London you'd be careful remember."

Rose didn't argue and sat quietly for the rest of the journey, thinking about everything that had happened since her birthday, just over a month ago. Two people were dead and a body that had lain undiscovered since just after Christmas had been identified as a murder victim. It was Easter when she had started asking questions about Constance's death. Stuart wouldn't have fitted into Constance and Harry's set, although he was a gambler. So maybe through the horses? Musselburgh had a racetrack. Harry had been part owner of two horses who had probably raced there. Is that how he might have known Stuart? She closed her eyes and was almost asleep when she remembered the dream about Troy shooting horses. The thought gave her a start when she remembered Troy had bought into a racing syndicate. Why hadn't she remembered that before.

"God I'm an idiot," she muttered under her breath as she typed a text to Rob.

Do you remember anything about the day Troy took us racing in Doncaster? Who was there?

Don't remember much. I have a couple of photos, I think. Somewhere on an old phone.

Can you look them out? Let's meet later. I have an idea.
Can't tonight. Sorry, I got a gig and a date.
No worries, just ping me the photos if you find them.
:-) on it.

"Everything alright Rose?"

"Yeah, it is. I think some of the puzzle is starting to come together."

.oOo.

The A & E department at Edinburgh Infirmary was quiet. The banks of chairs were sparingly filled with patients waiting to be seen, but despite the calm, the clerk gave Rose a welcome worthy of Nurse Ratchet. "This isn't the right place, you should have gone to your doctor's surgery. I can't prioritise you. You may have a long wait."

Rose put her hand up, she wasn't about to get into an argument with the woman. Who knows what sort of a day she had had, Rose thought. A&E must be a nightmare to work in. "You don't have to wait Anthony, if you want to try and see Hickson."

"I've just called her, she won't have time to get back to the station today, but she's going to call me. She's out by the coast somewhere, the connection wasn't great. I'll go and get us some tea. I don't know about you, but I am really hungry."

"Me too, that piece of toast was a long time ago."

While Anthony was away Rose started to redraw her map. This time she included Troy and Stuart. She was almost finished when Rob's text pinged in with a couple of photographs. One was of her and Troy, the other was of Troy and a group of men standing in a semicircle with their thumbs up. The man in the centre was holding a rosette. It was Harry Turnbull. She thought back to the day. Why hadn't she recognised the man when she'd delivered the lunch for Constance? Was knowing Troy the reason Harry got in touch with her?

Any use?

Oh yeah. Harry Turnbull, standing next to Troy, holding the Rosette.

Really? He looks different from the obit photo in the paper.

Ten years younger. I don't know how I missed this.

Stuart's not there though.

No.

You think Harry was using you somehow. Telling Troy about your shop?

I don't know. But I intend to find out.

Rose sent Mike the photograph from the racetrack and asked him to see if there was any record of Harry Turnbull visiting Troy in prison.

Anthony came back with some watery looking tea and packets of crisps. "For a hospital, the snacks leave a lot to be desired. No sandwiches and I wouldn't insult you with the cakes they had on offer."

Rose waved her hand and verbally launched into a tirade about the photo of Harry with Troy, Rob sent. "What if Harry contacted me because Troy asked him to, because they were cooking something up against me?"

"First Stuart - if it was Stuart we saw - and now Harry, both with a connection to Troy. But your ex is in prison."

"Yeah, in prison and full of hate. I wouldn't put anything past him. He's always said I should watch out."

Anthony frowned. "But why now. What set this off? And how do that other pair fit in, and Mathers, and the murders? Troy couldn't have had anything to do with that."

"I'm convinced William Summers didn't know me from Adam when I met him in Chelsea, whatever Troy is up to. But if there's money missing, laundered or stolen somehow, Troy would know how to do it. And Stuart, he's capable of murder. I know that for a fact."

Anthony was about to ask her what she meant, when a nurse appeared, shouting, "Rose McLaren?" from the other end of the patient waiting area.

.oOo.

Anthony's printer was almost out of ink by the time the last photograph was printed. They had stopped at a craft shop on the way back to his flat to pick up a roll of white paper. Anthony had attached the paper along one of the walls in the living room. Rose was writing the names of each person they had a photograph or press cutting for in a straight line at the top of the paper.

Constance Brown
Harry Turnbull
Donna Meikle
Victoria ? and ?
Mathers
William Summers
Stuart Dunphy
Troy Aitkins

With a series of coloured lines she connected them into different relationships. Friends, Family, acquaintances, business partners and put a star next to the three who were dead. Then she highlighted Mathers and Victoria and her brother.

"What about Andrea Summers

"Surely you don't think Andrea has anything to do with the murders? Andrea was afraid something might happen to her."

"I know, but something she said, I can't remember what, it seems important."

"And you need to eat," Anthony pointed at the unopened box of sushi and the remains of the Japanese take-away they had ordered. "Never had this before, it's good Rose, really good."

Rose smiled. "Your neat bachelor flat is a bit of a tip now, I'm sorry." The once orderly living room was indeed untidy. To fix the paper on the wall Anthony had had to take down a couple of pictures and move some furniture around.

"At least it feels lived in. Under any other circumstances I would say it was a pleasure to have you as a guest. But ..."

"I can't thank you enough for everything. You've helped me to stay strong. When Kay phoned me about dad, I just wanted to give up."

Chapter 19

Rose and Anthony stayed up into the small hours talking about her father, Troy, and her struggle with addiction. Although he already knew a lot about her, he patiently listened as she went through the stages of her life. Leaving the RAF, moving in with Troy, addiction, prison (because of Troy), the shop, Anthony had taken her fears seriously. She crossed her arms and gave herself a hug. Anthony was moving about in the kitchen, the aroma of cinnamon and coffee tempted her out of bed.

"Tea madame, and lookie here."

"Oooh, those look really yum," she said as Anthony pulled a baking sheet from the oven with hot baked cinnamon rolls.

"I wasn't brave enough to try out your pain au chocolat recipe."

"Ha ha, I'm not sure if even Trixie has tried that out yet. I'm longing to get back into the kitchen, but this thing is on for another two weeks apparently." She tapped the cast on her arm. "I'm going to call Sally, try and talk to her. Did you speak to Hickson, I don't remember her calling back yesterday."

"She didn't, I guess she's on another investigation. But this one will be an ongoing case for her too. I'll try her again today. Want me to drive you to Sally's?"

"No, I think I feel well enough to get about. I have a long journey tomorrow, I need to get back to being independent. Thanks for last night. Talking about the past, my Dad, it really helped."

"My pleasure, you can ask me anytime you need support. With your Dad gone, and I know you didn't have the opportunity to talk to him, maybe I can …" Anthony paused and turned away to wipe his eyes.

"Oh come here, you wonderful man." Rose gave him a hug.

"Enough, I don't know what came over me," Anthony pulled himself upright and stepped back. Since his marriage had ended he was unused to allowing his feelings to get the better of him. He cleared his throat. "Do you want to stay here tonight, before you go to Bristol tomorrow?"

"If that's alright with you, yes please. After all, the master plan is on your wall. Can you live with it for a few days, until I'm back from Bristol? I'll go back to the flat and sort out some different clothes, Trixie forgot to pack anything suitable for the service on Friday."

.oOo.

She sipped on the fresh coffee Anthony had brought her and turned on her laptop. Mike had had no luck identifying the man with Mathers and Victoria. But he had found another picture of Victoria in Musselburgh. This time she was with Stuart, her brother and Harry Turnbull at the racecourse. The caption was *another winner for Harry.* The picture had been taken after Constance's accident. Did Harry know this girl while she was working at the stables? If so, it meant he also knew she had changed her name. So far she had had three jobs and kept changing her name. Working at the stables,, working for Harry calling herself Janice and recently, using the name Victoria, when she'd started working at the shop.

Rose looked across at the wall of photographs, then back into her laptop. She searched for the family tree's she had created when she was in Bristol. And there it was, why hadn't she remembered? Constance's cousin had the same family name through marriage as Stuart. The name Dunphy.

Rose studied the photograph of the cousin and her children taken ten years before. The older girl would be about thirty now, but the middle one, the one next to a boy who looked almost the same age would be about twenty three. Victoria told Trixie she was twenty three and the man with Mathers looked about the same age. She checked the children's names against the information from the site. The middle children were twins, Willow and Devon Dunphy. There was an anomaly in the record. All the children's names were recorded in the family tree, but Willow and Devon were not shown as a direct descendant of the mother and father. Rose tapped her pen on her notepad, cursing herself for not paying attention to the details before; Willow and Devon Dunphy were adopted. Rose got up and drew a familial line on the paper, between Stuart and Constance's Canadian family with a star next to the twins. The twins were obvious not identical but there were facial similarities, she could see that now when she looked at the picture of the girl at the stables. They didn't look like the younger child, nor the young woman in the photograph either. Rose was about to call Anthony and tell him what she had put together, then hesitated. She sent Mike a text with a photograph of Stuart.

Any chance you can get a contact number for him, name of Stuart Dunphy?

Sure you want to contact him? From what I know of him, he's not a good guy?

Yeah I know

.oOo.

It took Mike less than an hour to get back to her with information about Stuart. He didn't have a number but his intel had given him an address of a nightclub he owned in Edinburgh. The club was not far from Anthony's flat.

"Just heading out, I'll see you later," Rose called and slipped out the door before Anthony could respond. He'd know she was lying about where she was going if he saw her. The club was locked when she got there, but there was a side door and a window which was slightly open. Peering through the window Rose saw the stairs led to a room above the club. She tapped on the door and then called through the window. "Hello, is anyone here?"

A plump woman in her twenties wearing a tight fitted midriff top and spanx leggings clattered down the stairs. She opened the door, leaving the chain in place. "Wha' ye want?" She said while chewing a bright blue ball of something sticky. The blue gum, contrasting with the pouty red lips, made her look like a cartoon.

"I'm looking for Stuart."

The woman looked her up and down. "Yer nae his type hen. I'd take a hike if Ah wis ye."

Rose pulled herself straight and looked the woman in the eye. "Tell him Rose, Rose McLaren wants to talk to him. He'll see me."

Rose's assertiveness had no impact on the woman, she rolled her eyes. "Mebee, he would, but he's nae here. Ah'll be sure tae tell him though."

Rose stepped away from the door just as a blue Mercedes pulled up outside. Stuart was driving. He removed his sunglasses and raised his eyebrows when he saw her, then whistled. "The lovely Rose McLaren, what are you doing here? Been in the wars love?" He cocked his head on one side taking her in while he locked the vehicle and swaggered round the car, next to where she was standing.

"Long time no see sweetheart," he said loudly then bending down, brought his face towards her and hissed in her ear. "You're quite a piece of work Rose. Making up stories, getting my friend locked up."

"Your friend who murdered my mother and tried to kill me you mean?"

He leaned back against the car and pulled out a packet of cigarettes. "What do you want, Rose. Why are you here?"

"I have some questions. But if we're going to talk, we need some ground rules."

"Oh you're a funny lady." He jabbed his finger towards her face. "I'm the one who makes the rules around here Rose."

The door next to the club swung open, the woman in spanx called out, "Is everything alright?"

"Yeah, put the kettle on, strong and black. We have a visitor."

Rose hesitated. "Can't we talk here, outside?"

Stuart shook his head and shrugged. "One chance Rose, take it or blow it, up to you."

Stuart lit the cigarette and blew out a ring of smoke as he started walking towards the building. He was about to close the door when Rose made a snap decision to join him inside.

"Alright, but people know I'm here, and they'll look for me." At least Mike knew where she would have gone if anything happened.

"Sure they will Rose. Sure they will."

Rose tapped her phone to silent and pressed the record button, whatever Stuart had to say she didn't want to be the only one who heard it. Then she followed Stuart upstairs, pulling the door behind her, without clicking the lock.

"Shut the door Rose. We don't want unwanted visitors now do we?" He strode two steps at a time to the top of the wooden stairs and turned right. His footsteps resounded on the bare wood floor. Directly ahead Rose could see spanx pouring hot water into a cafetiere. The room she was in had a cement floor, half fitted with kitchen units. A large pair of scales sat on a formica table, next to a hotplate, attached to an industrial grade extension cord. A fridge, a washing machine and a microwave on another table lined the wall opposite the cabinets. "He's in the office, down there," she pointed to a room further down the corridor with the door open. There were two other doors, one on either side of the corridor which were closed. One of the doors had a padlock and chain attached to a brace on the wall. Stuart was sitting behind a large wooden desk on a swivel chair. Each wall of the room was covered in shelves stacked with folders. The window blind was pulled down. The room smelled of stale cigarettes and sweat.

Stuart put his feet up on the desk in front of him as Rose entered. She sat down on one of the chairs opposite and waited while spanx followed her and put a mug of coffee on the desk for him. Neither of them asked Rose if she wanted coffee. Stuart stubbed out the cigarette and put his hands behind his head.

"So Rose, why are you here?"

"I saw you yesterday, in Musselburgh. You were with a woman who calls herself Victoria, but I think you know her by her real name, Willow. William Summers and Willow's brother, Devon were also there."

"And," Stuart unclasped his hands and stirred the coffee.

"Are you related, you all have the same last name, Dunphy. The girl, Willow, tried to work for me? I want to know why. Is Troy behind all this, using you to spy on me?" Stuart started to laugh. The deep throated cackle lasted for over a minute before he leaned forward. "Oh Rose, you always were stupid, how he put up with you for so long is a mystery. Troy has bigger fish to fry nowadays.

Rose was about to retort when she glanced down and saw a black hoodie laying on top of a box next to the desk. It had a red triangle on the sleeve. She looked up and caught Stuart's eye. He knew she had seen the hoodie. "You're right, I shouldn't have come, I made a mistake. Sorry, I'll just leave."

"Angie," he clicked his fingers, "some juice for our guest."

The woman came in with a cup. "Enjoy," she hissed as she stretched out her arm towards Rose who had got up from the chair.

"Come on Rose, be nice, drink it down."

Rose looked back at Stuart, "I'm not thirsty," she said, grabbing the cup she threw it across the desk at Stuart, and turned to run. Stuart was already out from behind the desk, and made a grab for her. She raised her leg and kicked him hard in the groin. He winced and stumbled against the desk. Spanx tried to tackle Rose as she flew out of the door, but she wasn't quick enough. Rose pushed her over and headed back along the corridor, clattered down the stairs, running for her life. She could hear Stuart behind her. She wrestled with the lock and escaped outside. Slamming the door she prayed she could put enough distance between them to get away . Her heart felt as if it would burst as she ran. Turning a corner she looked down the street, made a dash into the back garden of the nearest house and ducked behind a wooden shed.

Her fingers trembled as she pressed the dial pad on her phone to call Rob. But the call went to voicemail. She tried Anthony, his number went to voicemail too.

She could hear Stuart's voice and the voice of the woman. They were getting closer, they were shouting her name from the street. She held her breath at the sound of footsteps crunching the gravel on the path into the garden, there was nowhere else to hide.

"Hey who are you?" An unfamiliar voice called out.

"Just looking for my dog."

"Well it's not in here, so I suggest you do one."

"Can I look behind the shed?"

"There's nae dog there pal."

"Ok, no bother. Sorry."

Rose released the breath, surprised that Stuart had given up. She felt faint and dizzy.

"You alright?" The unfamiliar voice said.

Rose looked up. A fit thirty-something man was peering at her from the side of the shed. "I saw you run in, you looked scared, he was chasing you right? Should we call the police?"

Rose shook her head. "Thank you, I was trying to call a friend, but it went to voicemail. You were brave, he's a piece of work."

"I could tell that."

"Come into the house, you look really shaken up."

He walked with her back up the garden and through the rear glass doors.

"You're very kind, I must look quite shocking with ..."

"You're not exactly a vision. Look, are you sure you don't need the police or an ambulance?"

"No, these injuries are from last week. I am on the mend. My name's Rose by the way." She let out a sigh.

"Glad I could help you out Rose ... I think ... Is there any danger of him coming back? I have kids."

"No, he won't trouble you, I'm sure. I am going to talk to the police. They might ask you to witness what you saw, is that alright, or should I leave you out of it? He's connected to something else. You really don't need to worry."

"I hope so. Yes, leave me out of it, if you can. I think I'd prefer to forget what just happened this morning."

Rose sat in the back of the taxi counting her blessings. Bearding the lion in his own cage was best left for films and stories, not real life. Her choice to meet Stuart could have got her killed. Anthony and Rob had both texted her to apologise for missing her call, asking if she was alright; she daren't tell either of them where she had been. But she could at least tell Hickson where she could find Stuart Dunphy. Rose knew a drugs lab when she saw one. That padlocked door had all the signs and the triangle on the hoodie, that wasn't a coincidence, she knew that from Stuart's reaction.

Inspector Hickson was at the police station when Rose called. "You'd better come down straight away. I've just had Anthony on the phone as well, he's on his way over. I'm not sure what to think about you two, continuing to play detective."

Rose re-directed the taxi to the police station. Anthony was already there, waiting at the front desk for the inspector, by the time she arrived. "So where did you go?"

"You'll hear soon enough, when we talk to Hickson. It was dumb, but at least some good might have come out of it. I'm hoping Hickson can now go and arrest Stuart Dunphy."

"For what?"

"Drugs lab and there was a hoodie, the same logo that I remembered seeing on the man who attacked me."

"You think Stuart was the person who attacked you?"

"No, probably one of the people he hires, he doesn't get to get his own hands dirty, although I think he was prepared to go there today."

"Rose! Why on earth did you go there alone for goodness sake."

"Not the smartest move, I'll admit."

Inspector Hickson arrived to take them to an interview room. She had been there before, when Anthony was a DCI. Hickson's expression foretold how the meeting would go. Rose braced herself for the inevitable cold shower of words and admonition.

"Your activity this morning Rose just cost a lot of money and wasted months of police surveillance. Stuart Dunphy has already gone, so thanks for that."

Rose looked over at Anthony. He was shaking his head.

"But, he couldn't have taken everything so quickly."

"He was already on the move, we knew that, we just didn't know where to."

Chapter 20

"So that didn't go so well," said Rose as she and Anthony left the police station.

"No Rose, it didn't."

"Are you alright,?"

"Frankly, no. I'm angry at the stunt you pulled. Not only have you managed to interfere in a major police operation you could have been badly hurt, again, or worse. You said yourself that Stuart was capable of murder."

"I , well I realise it wasn't … it's just when I connected the name, Dunphy to the family in Canada, I … I couldn't stop thinking that if I confronted Stuart, I could figure out everything else too. I knew if I told you, you would have stopped me going over there."

Anthony stared at her. His eyes were cold. "Yes, you're right. I would have."

Rose swallowed hard. "I need to get my stuff ready for tomorrow. Would it be better if I stayed at my flat tonight?"

Anthony looked up towards the sky. The grey clouds overhead reflected the unpredictability of his fondness for Rose. He wanted to be a friend, a listener, a guide if she needed one, but she was damn difficult to like sometimes. She had caught him up in unprofessional behaviour, doing things he would never have sanctioned in a million years when he had been in the force. Her logical mind coupled with her illogical behaviour was stressing him out. He needed to put some boundaries between them, go back to having privacy and space. "I'm sorry, I can't be …, I'm not Rob."

"I know and if it's any consolation he used to get mad with me too. I get it. I'll need to come back with you and pack up what's there, if that's OK. Or you can just put them in a cab, and send them over."

"No, don't be silly. Of course you need to come back and get what's at mine. But can we agree not to discuss Constance Brown anymore?"

"Sure. Mind if I roll up the paper we started and take it away with the photo's?"

"Go ahead. It's all yours."

Anthony made coffee while Rose collected everything together. Neither of them said much, it was hard to ignore the elephant in the room as Rose rolled up the sheet of paper and collated the rest of the photographs he had printed out. The name Dunphy seemed to be indelibly printed within both of their minds for different reasons. Rose stared at the picture of the children in the Dunphy family photograph. Victoria had told Trixie she could work in the UK because she had a British passport. Was that what had upset Donna Meikle when she saw the photograph, had she thought Rose knew the children were not related by blood and were adopted? And if so, whose children were they? She had asked Stuart the wrong questions and now she had blown the chance she had to figure it out.

"Rose ... are you alright?"

"Yes, sorry just got lost in something that ... well, I'm not going to say, we agreed not to talk about it. I'll call a cab and be out of your hair as quickly as I can. Is it alright if I borrow this book though?" She pointed to the book on poison lying on the coffee table.

"Go ahead. Are you sure you'll be ok at the flat, and travelling down to Bristol tomorrow?"

"Yes, I will. I'm sure. Are we still friends?"

"Of course. I'm just an old fashioned fuddy duddy who can't quite manage your lack of control, exuberance, I don't know how to explain it."

"But your way, your methodical attitude, sometimes I wish I was more like that. I guess it's good we're all different."

He smiled. She was maddening but it was hard to stay cross with her for long. "I should drive you to Corstorphine. You'll never manage on your own at the other end with that cast on your arm."

"The driver will help, I'm a good tipper. The traffic will be terrible and you look done in. Take a rest and I'll let you know how things go down in Bristol."

.oOo.

Rose looked around at her flat, Rob's tidying meant she could relax and would be able to go to bed without having to make it up. She unrolled the ream of white paper from Anthony's and laid it out across the living room floor. What else had she missed? She began to redraw the flight plan map, this time she assumed the twins were born in the UK and had been moved to Canada. That would explain the British passport. There had to be records of international adoptions, but she doubted even Mike would be able to access names of children and who they were adopted by. But on passenger lists, if they'd been taken to Canada, there had to be a record of the two children's names on travel documents somewhere.

She sent a text to Mike.

The children in the Canadian photo. I think the middle 2 r adopted and might have been born in the UK. Any ideas how 2 find out, travel docs, passports?

U r out of luck on that one Rose. I've no idea where 2 start. If they were adopted as babies they would be on whoever was their guardian's travel docs.

Right, so it's hopeless?

Yeah, sorry.

She was about to take a shower when she remembered something Andrea had told her, Constance had had to take a break from eventing and missed out competing in an Olympics. She checked the dates of the Olympics on a Wikipedia page. Constance won her first Olympic medal when she was twenty and competed in the next four Olympic games. She had qualified to compete in the next games but pulled out at short notice when she was forty. Rose calculated the dates. Willow and Devon were both twenty three. The numbers worked. If Constance had pulled out because she was pregnant, Willow and Devon could be Constance's children. If they were, had Harry known the girl he had employed was Constance's daughter? And what about the row outside Constance's flat? Rose sighed. She had raised more questions than she had found answers. And really, what was the point? She had alienated Anthony, caused worry and upset for Trixie and who knows what had happened to Sally.

.oOo.

Her mood remained sombre as she made her way to Bristol the following day. The train, like her mind, was full. She had forgotten to book a seat in advance, and people were standing. The choice was an aisle seat in a carriage full of families or paying to upgrade to first class. The guard was sympathetic as she shelled out for the price of the upgrade. "Sorry hen."

"My fault, I should have booked. Where is everybody going?"

The guard shook his head, "Nae idea, Ah'm hoping there's nae trouble."

"Me too, although trouble seems to be following me these days."

Rose tapped her phone, she had tried to shut out all the questions from last night, but her mind kept spinning. She leaned her head back against the headrest and closed her eyes. She had removed the eye shield before she left home that morning. Apart from the cast and a light bruise on her face, there were few visible signs of her injuries, but she still felt weak. The impact on her body yesterday, her lunge at Stuart and the fallout with Anthony felt equal to being punched. She had just dropped into a sleep when her phone pinged with a text from Andrea Summer

Have you heard from William?
No. Should I have?

My son called me. William didn't come back from Scotland. I thought he'd gone to meet you.

I did see him from a distance, he doesn't know that though. He was in bad company.

Typical William he always finds it. Where?

Musselburgh, at Harry's house

!!? I'm really worried about the kids. I'm coming back to the UK later this afternoon

OK, Where will you go? Do you want a number for an Inspector in Edinburgh?

Maybe, I'll contact you when I get back. I'm gonna kick that woman out of my house

I thought you'd signed it over to William?

I've had some other advice. That document, it's not even legal. Mathers was struck off fifteen years ago for fraud in an investments scam. Can you believe it!

Wow! I'm heading to Bristol. My father's cremation.

:-(Rose I'm so sorry

Thanks. Do you have a number for William. I want to ask him about last weekend.

Sure. Here it is …

Rose saved the number that Andrea sent her. *Keep me posted when you get back.*

I will. Take care Rose

Rose put her phone on the table, she was right, trouble followed her. Every time she tried to stop thinking about what might have happened to Constance Brown, something nudged her to think about it all over again.

She checked the time and remembered she had forgotten to phone Kay and confirm when she was arriving.

"Hey, I'm on the train, should be there by 5.30pm. It's packed, so I had to travel first class again. I can feel my Dad's finger wagging about wasting his money."

"It's your money now Rose and I'm sure he'd prefer you to be comfortable than stand most of the way."

"True. Do you mind if we go over to his house later? I know I said I didn't want to, but there's something of his I'd like to take with me to the cremation."

"No problem. I'm off this afternoon. I'll pick up some food we can eat on the way there. Unless you're full from train food."

"No, just coffee and a sandwich. See you later, thanks Kay."

She willed herself to try and relax, focus on her Dad and the cremation service. The train was still busy and she hadn't been able to get back to sleep. **(leave in)**

"Salad with hummus or bean and guacamole taco?" asked Kay as they sat in the car outside the station. "You've bought the Scottish weather with you."

Rose nodded, staring through the window as the rain splashed onto the screen.

"Either one, I'm not that hungry right now. Do you need me to navigate?"

"I'm alright from here, I know Nailsea quite well, just when we get closer."

"How are you? And don't say 'fine', I can see that you're not."

"OK the other version of fine, you know it? It ends with neurotic?"

Kay smiled. "Yeah, yeah, sorry."

"It will pass, and hopefully once the service is over, I'll have a clearer idea about my future." Rose slumped back in her seat and stared out of the passenger window for the rest of the journey.

.oOo.

It wasn't until Rose walked into the living room that she realised someone had broken in. The back patio door had been forced open and was half hanging on its hinge. Her father's desk was covered in papers and there were files from his business all over the floor. She ran upstairs, the bedrooms hadn't been disturbed except for hers. Someone had spray painted *nowhere to run* on the wall by her bed.

"I've called the police," said Kay. "What does that mean?"

"It's a message, it's from Troy."

"Troy? The chap who's in prison, your ex?"

"Yeah. We used to sing that, when we first got together, it was a joke between us. I was right. Troy has been using Stuart to get to me, maybe even Harry and somehow he managed to involve the Dunphy kids."

"The who kids?"

"It's a long story, but I have a feeling I have worked it out."

"OK, well the police have just arrived, you can tell them."

Chapter 21

The police officers promised to follow up with Inspector Hickson, but Rose knew from the Edinburgh Fringe case that cross border communication between the different forces wasn't simple. She was taking a shower at Kay's when something that had been bothering her about Constance clicked into place. Wrapped in a fluffy blue bath sheet she lay back on the bed until all the pieces seemed to fit together. She pulled the notebook out of her bag and created a final map. She hoped Mike could help track down the paperwork she'd need to prove her theory. Then she called Anthony and told him what had happened at her father's house.

"I've pinged you a picture of the wall. Troy has to be behind it. You can check with Rob, everyone used to joke about our song, we even did a karaoke together in a pub once. He probably paid Stuart, or Stuart paid someone."

"And nothing was missing?"

"No, not even Dad's medals, which is what I had gone to the house to collect. Not that they are worth much to anyone else."

"I didn't realise he was in the forces."

"Army, that's where he learned how to fix cars. He did active service in the Falklands. His Army experience was one of the reasons he was so against me going into the RAF."

"Can you speak to Hickson, and let her know what's happened. I don't think the Bristol police are going to act on it very quickly and I don't expect she wants to hear from me."

"Of course, you know from the work we did together on the Fringe murders cross regional policing isn't straight forward."

"Yeah. Look, I know we weren't going to talk about it, but I also have an idea about what happened to Constance and Harry and Donna."

"Surely you don't think Troy is behind any of that?"

"No, and I think that's what's made figuring things out so hard. Two things were happening at the same time, it's only today that I realised what was happening to me had nothing to do with what happened to Constance Brown. I'm hoping Mike can track down some paperwork, and I need to speak to William Summers, when he turns up."

"William Summers? He's missing?"

"According to Andrea. She flew back to London this afternoon. She's worried about the kids, they're at boarding school, and they were supposed to spend this weekend with their Dad. Only he didn't come back from Scotland. My guess is he's at Donna's house."

"Why?"

"That's what I want to speak to him about. Did you ever hear from Mathers by the way?"

"No."

"Me neither. Andrea told me he was suspended for fraud years ago. His practice isn't legit."

"Rose, I will let Hickson know about what's happened in Bristol, but I'm not going to mention anything about Constance Brown, I'd still really prefer not to get involved anymore. But I would urge you to tell her everything you know or think you have figured out. Don't try any more heroics."

"Sure. Thanks, and no bother, I just wanted to let you know."

"OK, I hope Friday goes well. See you back in Edinburgh. Take care."

While Rose was on the call, Kay had brought in a tray with a steaming mug of tea, some of the biscuits from Rose's shop and three blue glass tincture bottles with handwritten labels. She moved to sit next to Rose and watched her savour the dunked shortbread in her tea.

"I have to say our shortbread is damn delicious," Rose said, turning towards Kay. "What's in the bottles?"

"Thought you might like a muscle rub?"

"Thanks, that would be lovely. My neck and shoulders feel tight, weighed down. I haven't exercised or done anything for my body since the mugging."

"And your mind hasn't stopped since we first met. Your Dad, the attack and trying to figure out a suspicious death, three of them, you need to relax Rose."

Kay picked up the three tiny phials and gave them to Rose to smell. Frankincense, Geranium and Bergamot "Which one?"

Rose chose the Bergamot. Kay dabbed a tiny spot of the oil behind Rose's neck and began moving her hands across her neck and shoulders, pushing and pulling and kneading her knuckles into some of the pressure points. The subtle scent from the essential oil permeated the bedroom. Rose closed her eyes and allowed her mind to let go, while Kay worked her magic on the physical tension.

When Kay left Rose dressed for bed, and studied her map. This time she connected Constance, Willow and Devon to Harry, drew an arrow north and wrote Canada and the year, the same year Constance hadn't competed in the Olympics. She added another line, this time from Constance to Canada and a different date December 30th, the day Constance told everyone she was flying out to Canada, to meet her cousin.

She sent a text to Mike

Another travel question, I think Constance Brown was booked to go out to Canada. I always thought that that part of the story was weird. Any thoughts, how to find out if there was a booking?

You think she was booked and didn't travel, so passengers lists?

Yeah, they said for Hogmanay, she was heading out. So anywhere from December 30th. And another passenger, coming this way, probably a month later, just before Constance died. Barrie Dunphy.

Her cousin?

Yeah.

I'll see what I can do. I'll have to ask a favour.

I'm in your debt - thanks x

! Big time you are :-)

It was almost 11 by the time Rose was happy with her map. And now she needed to talk to William Summers. She called Donna Meikle's home number. She had already tried him several times on the mobile number Andrea had given her, but he hadn't answered.

She was about to give up when someone picked up the receiver.

"Hello, is that you. Where are you?"

"Hello William. Who were you expecting? This is Rose McLaren, we met in London."

The man sighed, "Oh yeah, I remember you. How did you know I was here?"

"Ah, well I'm good at finding people. I'm guessing you're trying to find the paper trail. Donna's rural house was the perfect place to hide everything. What I don't understand is why you stayed there. You must realise you're in danger."

"What do you mean?"

"Whoever you're expecting just might not be the person who turns up." Rose was bluffing, she needed to get him to talk but if she was right, William was in danger. According to Mike, Barrie Dunphy had landed at Glasgow, three hours ago.

"How do you know I'm expecting anyone?"

"Barrie Dunphy, Constance Brown's cousin was having an affair with your sister. You need to find those papers before he does."

William gasped. "How do you know all this?"

"I can try and help, if you'll help me." Rose was about to explain when she heard glass breaking. "William, are you alright?" But there was no answer. She could hear the sounds of a scuffle and flesh on flesh, whoever was there was either hitting William or the other way round. "William," she called again, but the phone went dead. She phoned Inspector Hickson.

Kay was standing at the bedroom door listening. She had come by to say goodnight when she heard Rose on the phone to William. "What's happening Rose?"

"Potentially another murder, but I hope not. If the police get there on time, they might just save him."

"Who?"

"William Summers."

"You've figured it all out haven't you?" Kay said, pointing to the open notebook with Rose's map and her notes.

"Yeah, and if I wasn't so blind I could have gone there a lot quicker."

"You can still see Rose."

"For how much longer Kay. Look, she pulled up the photo of the Canadian Cousin and his family in Canada and tapped on the face of the younger man." It's Stuart Dunphy, Troy's friend."

"Troy's behind all this, killing your customers?"

"No, that's what made it all so difficult. It's what I was trying to explain to Anthony earlier. There are two different crimes. Revenge against me by Troy, the other is all about money, greed and secrets. They became linked because Stuart is involved with them both."

"Sorry, I'm lost Stuart murdered you customers, and this William?"

"No, the murderer is this man, Barrie Dunphy, Constance's cousin."

Rose's phone started ringing. It was Inspector Hickson. I thought you'd want to know that Perth Police managed to get there on time. William Summers is injured but he'll be alright. I'm going to need another statement from you Rose. When are you back?

"Friday, late though, after the cremation. Is Saturday alright?"

"Sure, come to the station. About 10am, does that work?"

"Yes. Any news about Stuart?"

"Yes. He got a bit careless. We caught him at the ferry port trying to leave the country. He's trying to wriggle off the hook, so he's given up the others, trying to make a deal. We can talk about that on Saturday. I have spoken to the police in Bristol, I think they're onside about sharing information."

"The others, you mean Willow and Devon? But not Troy?"

"Oh no, him too."

"Thanks, that's brilliant, I didn't see that coming."

"Rest up Rose, you've had quite a time of it. But Anthony warned me, you wouldn't give up."

Rose laughed. It was the first time she had spoken to Hickson without feeling like a scolded school girl. She closed her eyes and breathed in. The aroma from the essential oil was still in the air, she savoured it and leaned back on the pillow.

"Are you OK, need anything?"

"No, a good sleep and a day of doing nothing tomorrow, if that's alright. Maybe a walk, but I just want to veg."

"Then veg you shall, I have food in, there's nothing you need to do. Sleep well."

She watched as Kay glided quietly out of the room. Her soothing presence lingered as Rose, breathing evenly, fell into a deep sleep.

Chapter 22

The service for her father went smoothly and as Rose said her final goodbye's to him she experienced a deep peace in her mind and in her body. "Bye Dad," she whispered softly as she walked with Kay through the grounds of the crematorium.

"All will be well Rose, please don't forget me. Now your father has gone, there's probably no reason for you to come back here very often after you've sold the house. But you're always welcome to stay with me if you'd like to."

"Oh Kay, of course I want to keep in touch. You know we never really talked about that night when I told you about the money. I know what you said to me in the hospital, but …"

Kay closed her eyes, she remembered only too well and hated herself for it. "And now isn't the time, not after today and saying goodbye to your father."

"Can you give me a clue what it was about?"

"Can we save that for next time?"

"OK, but as you know, I don't give up on puzzles." She bent down to give Kay a hug before heading onto the station platform. "Thank you for everything."

.oOo.

Her own flat felt bare and plain in contrast to Kay's when she arrived home. "Walls, you need a paint job," she said aloud, wondering if the time had come to really make Edinburgh her home and buy somewhere. She could afford to do that now. The neutral tones, the white walls, her beige sofa had seemed so right, but now she was ready for colour, to be a bit more adventurous, and expand the shop.

She was still upbeat the following morning. The service for her father, the way he had planned it had strangely settled her. She had no trepidation about meeting Hickson as she made her way over to the police station from the shop with a box of muffins and some fresh coffee.

"So ye are going tae fill us all in wi' wha's been going on?" said Trixie as she made up the box of muffins for Rose.

"Yes, later. Are you and Graham free to come for dinner tonight at mine? I've invited Rob. Marion and Mike, it'll be like a second birthday party, but without cake, and the food will be take-out. Pizza and Thai"

"Yum, is Anthony coming too?"

"Yes, but we'll see if he actually turns up. He hasn't texted back yet. He and I fell out a bit. I'm hoping it's mended but I'm not sure."

Inspector Hickson sat patiently while Rose described what she had found in Bristol and heard on the phone call when she spoke to William Summers. "Stuart has given us a statement and we have found evidence that Troy discovered you were going to inherit money from your Dad."

"Maybe that's what started him off, but he had always threatened revenge."

"Well, hopefully Troy will be charged if we're successful in making a case. Certainly, Stuart is facing jail time, although less than if he hadn't talked."

"What about what happened to Constance, Harry and Donna?"

"Barrie is in custody for attacking William Summers. We haven't found Willow or Devon, but it won't be long before they're caught. We have informed all the ports and airlines to be on the lookout for them in case they try to leave the country. Based on what you've told me, and the evidence from the lab, I'm very hopeful Barrie will be charged with murder as well as assault. You know we can't use any of the emails you sent me, but we're confident there's more to be found that we can use. I'm not going to flatter you and say well done, we would have got there." Hickson picked up the file and neatened the stack of papers. There was still a chill in the air between them, but Rose sensed the beginning of a thaw.

.oOo.

"So come on, don't leave us hanging on any longer. What is the story and how on earth did you figure it out?" said Rob, polishing off the last of the Thai spring rolls. The gathering of her tribe had started early and everyone was in high spirits, glad to have 'their Rose' back.

"It's all on here, she said pointing to the roll of paper she had fixed on the wall behind the sofa. I only started to see the whole picture after Mike called in a favour, then it all fit together."

"Slainte Mhath Mike," said Trixie, mimicking herself from Rose's birthday two months earlier and holding up a bottle of Irn Bru.

Rose was about to tell the story when the doorbell rang. It was Anthony.

"Sorry I'm late."

"Aww and Rob's been a wee piggy and no' left ye any spring rolls."

"There's plenty of other food. I'm so glad you came," said Rose, accepting the huge bunch of flowers he was carrying.

"Inspector Hickson is singing your praises. I hope I'm not too late for the big reveal."

"Make yourselves comfy everyone, it's quite the tale, two of them in fact."

Her guests spread themselves out on the sofas and beanie bags.

"At the beginning, the story about Constance going to Canada, didn't make sense. She had been alone in her flat for two years, after the accident. Why would she suddenly decide to take a trip across the other side of the world? Her neighbours talked to me about her change in personality, and then seeing her hair a different colour. The vet told us the accident with the horse was caused by yew and I began to wonder if Constance too had been poisoned. Yew doesn't cause hair loss, but Thallium does. It's known as the poisoner's poison. Hickson had already told Anthony a lab report showed abnormal toxicology. Yesterday Hickson confirmed it was thallium."

"But Rose, why. Why was she killed?" Said Marion.

"I'm getting to that. Constance and Harry had been lovers for years, it was an on and off relationship. Constance didn't want to marry, but Harry remained faithfully in love with her. The same year she was supposed to compete in her fifth Olympics she found out she was pregnant. I am assuming here that Harry was the father. She chose to have the twins adopted by her cousin Barrie Dunphy and his wife; there was a financial arrangement, and a trust was set up for the twins. And here's where the two stories converge. Stuart Dunphy, a friend of my ex, was also Barrie's nephew."

"Wow, that's crazy," said Trixie.

"Yep, it is a small world after all, sometimes. What do they say about degrees of separation? Barrie was a financial advisor and big-wig in wealth management. He was also involved with property scams, fraud and money laundering. He mentored his nephew Stuart down the same path. When Stuart was almost caught in North America, Barrie set him up in the UK. I suspect that the twins were difficult children, they ended up in trouble with the police in Canada and Barrie sent them over to the UK to Stuart. They went along with whatever he wanted. When the twins turned twenty-one Barrie discovered the coffers of the trust for the twins were empty. Constance had drained them dry and used all the money for herself. This is what caused the row the neighbours saw in the front garden. What I don't understand is why Harry employed his daughter and played along with the name changes she used. But maybe he didn't know that the twins were his children. Barrie and Stuart hatched a plan to make sure the twins got what they were due. But Barrie wanted more. He wanted not just the money from the trust, he wanted all Constance's money. Stuart knew Mathers from prison, he was broke and willing to do anything – including property scams, forging ownership documents etc. Which is how the money went missing from the business. Barrie duped Harry into a property scam, with the help of Mathers.

"Mike managed to get a bunch of encrypted emails which prove Stuart bank rolled Mathers office and made up a phoney partner Mr Rooney, who was always away on business. Remember we're talking millions of pounds worth of property – the Morningside flats, Harry's London flats, swindling Andrea and William out of their Sloane Square house too. The twins also wanted revenge, Constance was after all their mother, and not only had she given them away at birth, but she had spent their trust fund as well – they probably see it as the ultimate rejection. They were in on Barrie's plans to kill Constance for revenge by creating the horse-riding accident. The twins, under instruction from Barrie (if you believe Stuart's version of events) then dosed her horse with yew, causing the horse to act erratically and eventually fall - but Constance survived the accident - so they had to come up with another plan for her eventual murder. It was the twins themselves who poisoned her – slowly. The postie told the police when she spoke to them about the boxes of chocolates she had delivered regularly. But of course, no one took any notice of that information until now. Then they found out about Harry's plan to take her on a cruise. They had to hurry her death up by breaking in and dripping poison into her mouth, leaving her to die on her own with no-one to know about it till weeks later."

"And Harry?"

"Harry had found out that Donna and Barrie Dunphy were having an affair. It had been going on for years, before she was widowed, and Harry had sent Donna letters accusing Barrie of having something to do with Constance's initial accident. Donna didn't know Barrie's adopted children were involved, when she told her lover about the letters. Harry realised immediately that Constance's eventual death was not an accident. He genuinely thought she had gone on the cruise. He was going to meet her in Hawaii. e put two and two together and confided his suspicions about Barrie to Mathers, not realising Mathers was working for both Stuart and Barrie. The week after Constance's body was found Barrie instructed the twins to get rid of Harry. and make it look like a suicide."

"Sorry, I still don't why they killed Donna?" Rob said..

"My guess is that after I showed her the photograph, she put things together and realised that the twins were doing Barrie's bidding. She started asking the right questions and the twins got spooked. Stuart said that it was Devon who drugged her, then they both pushed her off the road and into the Tay. They then drugged and kidnapped Sally in order to put Willow (Victoria) in her place and that way they could find out what I was up to and look for opportunities to mess with me – but Stuart took a more brutal approach beating me up and breaking into Dad's house in Bristol. When I didn't come back to work, Willow or Amy or Victoria, or Joanne, just disappeared again."

"Where does William Summers fit in all this?" Anthony had been quietly making notes and nodding as Rose shared her theory.

"What the twins didn't know at the time was that Donna had also told her brother William about the letters from Harry, accusing Barrie. When William went to meet Stuart and the twins in Musselburgh, he told them he was going to find his sister's letters and show them to the police. Like Donna he had no idea who was really behind Constance's accident. They told him to lay low at Donna's, and that they were on the trail of who killed Harry and Donna. William believed them.

"And throughout this all, Troy was also pulling Stuart's strings, and he had set the twins to follow me. Stuart has confessed everything in order to get a lighter sentence – how Troy persuaded him to mess with me, beat me up etc. Killing me would be too quick, far more important to make me suffer over and over again. I think they had actually planned to beat me up in Perth, but Devon realised I'd seen him and would recognise him again. I was playing right into Troy's hands, while I was trying to find out what happened to Constance. I do regret that my interference probably cost Donna her life though."

"So wha' are the twins noo? Ah hope they are banged up, reet?"

"No, I don't know if Stuart tipped them off but they got clean away, they are in the wind temporarily the police are looking for them.So it is only a matter of time before they are caught. Barrie and Stuart are in jail , and Troy will have time added onto his sentence."

Everyone was silent when Rose finished speaking. Marion leaned over to Mike and gave him a big smacker on the cheek. "Well done honey."

"Nah, it's all down to Rose, I just looked where she directed. God, money eh, talk about the root of evil."

Rose smiled, "Well talking of that, I do have some news which I hope will make you all happy for me. I've been trying to tell you all since I found out. But ..." she opened her hands and pulled a face, "... murder and crime just kept getting in the way. Before I talk anymore I'm going to make a big pot of tea and coffee and serve a little snack to go with it."

She lifted a napkin which had been covering a plate on a shelf behind the table, "Thanks to Trixie, look what we have! Voilà - Pain au Chocolat!"

Bake your own
Pain au chocolat:

Ingredients (for 8 servings)

- 4 cups flour(500 g)
- ½ cup water(120 mL)
- ½ cup milk(120 mL)
- ¼ cup sugar(50 g)
- 2 teaspoons salt
- 1 packet instant dry yeast
- 3 tablespoons unsalted butter, softened
- 1 ¼ cups cold unsalted butter(285 g), cut into ½-inch (1 cm) thick slices
- 1 egg, beaten
- 2 bars sweetened chocolate bar

Preparation

1. In a large bowl, mix the flour, water, milk, sugar, salt, yeast, and butter.

2. Once the dough starts to clump, turn it out onto a clean counter.

3. Lightly knead the dough and form it into a ball, making sure not to over-knead it.

4. Cover the dough with plastic wrap and refrigerate for one hour.

5. Slice the cold butter in thirds and place it onto a sheet of parchment paper..

6. Place another piece of parchment on top of the butter, and beat it with a rolling pin.

7. Keeping the parchment paper on the butter, use a rolling pin to roll the butter into a 7-inch (18 cm) square, ½-inch (1 cm) thick. If necessary, use a knife to trim the edges and place the trimmings back on top of the butter and continue to roll into a square.

8. Transfer the butter layer to the refrigerator.

9. To roll out the dough, lightly flour the counter. Place the dough on the counter, and push the rolling pin once vertically into the dough and once horizontally to form four quadrants.

10. Roll out each corner and form a 10-inch (25 cm) square.

11. Place the butter layer on top of the dough and fold the sides of the dough over the butter, enclosing it completely.

12. Roll the dough with a rolling pin to seal the seams, making sure to lengthen the dough, rather than widening it.

13. Transfer the dough to a baking sheet and cover with plastic wrap. Refrigerate for 1 hour.

14. Roll out the dough on a floured surface until it's 8x24 inches (20x61 cm).

15. Fold the top half down to the middle, and brush off any excess flour.

16. Fold the bottom half over the top and turn the dough clockwise to the left. This completes the first turn.

17. Cover and refrigerate for one hour.

18. Roll out the dough again two more times, completing three turns in total and refrigerating for 1 hour in between each turn. If at anytime the dough or butter begins to soften, stop and transfer back to the fridge.

19. After the final turn, cover the dough with plastic wrap and refrigerate overnight.

20. To form the croissants, cut the dough in half. Place one half in the refrigerator.

21. Flour the surface and roll out the dough into a long narrow strip, about 8x40 inches (20x101 cm).

22. With a knife, trim the edges of the dough.

23. Cut the dough into 4 rectangles.

24. Place the chocolate on the edge of the dough and roll tightly enclosing it in the dough.

25. Place the croissants on a baking sheet, seam side down.

26. Repeat with the other half of the dough.

27. Brush the croissants with the beaten egg. Save the rest of the egg wash in the fridge for later.

28. Place the croissants in a warm place to rise for 1-2 hours.

29. Preheat oven to 400°F (200°C).

30. Once the croissants have proofed, brush them with one more layer of egg wash.

31. Bake for 15 minutes or until golden brown and cooked through. Serve warm.

If you enjoyed

MURDER BY STEALTH

You can keep in touch with Liza and find out advance notice about her other work in progress. Sign up to a monthly newsletter (https://linktr.ee/lizamileswriter) or link to social media, Facebook, Twitter and Instagram here: www.lizamileswriter.com

Please do post a review or contact Liza via her website to let her know your comments. Liza's other works of fiction include:

- Murder on Morrison – A Rose McLaren Mystery
- Game of Murder – A Rose McLaren Mystery
- Love Bites
- My Life's Not Funny

Printed in Great Britain
by Amazon

16991417R00135